His Majesty's Elephant

Judith Tarr

· · · · · · · · · · · · ·

His Majesty's Elephant

Jane Yolen Books

Harcourt Brace & Company

San Diego   New York   London

Requests for permission to make copies of any part of
the work should be mailed to: Permissions Department,
Harcourt Brace & Company, 8th Floor,
Orlando, Florida 32887.

Library of Congress Cataloging-in-Publication Data
Tarr, Judith.
His Majesty's elephant/Judith Tarr.—1st ed.

p.   cm.

Summary: Charlemagne's daughter must call on
her own magic and the power of a young Breton and a special
elephant to save her father from a deadly Byzantine spell.
ISBN 0–15–200737–7
1. Charlemagne, Emperor, 724–814—Juvenile fiction.
[1. Charlemagne, Emperor, 724–814—Fiction.   2. Magic—Fiction.]
I. Title.
PZ7.T179Hi   1993
[Fic]—dc20   93-12878

Designed by Camilla Filancia
Printed in the United States of America
First edition   A B C D E

To

BRETT *and* JASON *and* SHENITA

His Majesty's Elephant

Prelude

· · · · · · · · · · · ·

HIS MAJESTY'S ELEPHANT was Abul
Abbas, gift of the Caliph Haroun al-Rashid to his
friend the Emperor Charlemagne. Along with him
came many other wonders, including a golden
Talisman containing a fragment of the True Cross
on which Jesus died. This Talisman was found by
Napoleon, tradition says, on the breast of the Emperor in his tomb, and hangs now, a gleam of gold
at the end of a long corridor, in the Tau Palace at
Rheims.

This much is history.

But suppose that the Talisman was more, and
that the Elephant had a part in its magic. . .

One

· · · · · · · · · · · · ·

*R*OWAN SAW the Elephant the day it came to Aachen. People had been talking about nothing else for days. It was vast, they said, like a rock rising out of the sea, and grey like one too, and its ears were like sails, and its snout like a snake, long and supple. The Caliph had sent it, a gift from the lord of the East to the Emperor of the West, and its coming toward Aachen was like a king's processional.

It was smaller than she had thought. That was the first thing she noticed. She stood among the princesses, right by the throne under its golden canopy, and watched the dark bearded men in their turbans and their silks, bearing gift after gift from their lord and master. The Elephant was the last. It filled the gate of the hall, a looming shadow; then it was inside, draped in silk and gold, and there were knobs of gold on its tusks. It was a splendid thing, but it was hardly bigger than a peasant's hut, and as its handlers prodded it down the long aisle, she thought that somehow it looked sad.

Her father stood up to greet the Elephant, which was

a mighty honor. It bowed down in front of him. That made him smile under the sweep of his mustache. Some people were afraid of the great strange thing—Gisela had fainted dead away, and the maids were quietly frantic—but the Emperor was delighted with the gift. His voice rang out over the buzz of the court, light and thin for a man so big, but pitched to carry. "Thank our friend and brother," he said, "and tell him that we shall treasure this most of all the riches he has given."

The Caliph's ambassador answered just as graciously. Then he added, "One gift yet remains, a little thing, but the Commander of the Faithful bade me bear it direct from his hand to your majesty's. His prayers and his blessing lie on it, and his hope that your majesty will cherish it as the gift of brother to brother."

The Emperor's brows rose. This was interesting. Rowan edged closer to the throne. Her sisters and their women stood in a knot, goggling at the Elephant. Once Rowan was free of them, she took a deep breath and leaned forward a little, the better to see what gift the Caliph sent his friend the Emperor.

The Caliph's ambassador took something from a fold of his robe, something wrapped in a shimmer of silk. He uncovered it carefully.

They had seen so much gold already—a kingdom's worth at least. But this was different. It was a pendant, perfectly round, as broad and deep as a child's palm. There were jewels round the rim, red and green and blue and white; and in the middle, a great cloudy crystal with a flaw in its center. The Caliph's man handled it with great respect, never touching it directly, but keeping it nested in the silk. "This," he said, "is a holy thing, a blessed Talisman set with a splinter of the Prophet Isa's Cross."

"The True Cross." The Emperor's voice was low, reverent. He held out his hand. The Caliph's man hesitated, then set the Talisman in it, still shielded in silk. The Emperor held it up. His face did not change expression, but Rowan thought she saw him start. As he held the Talisman, she could see the flaw more clearly. It was a splinter, as the infidel had said, set in the crystal as if it had grown there.

It made her desperately uneasy. She wanted to back away from it. At the same time she wanted to edge closer, to hold it in her hands. It would be heavy, she knew without knowing how, and smooth, and neither warm nor cold, but something in between. The holiness in it was proper Christian, even if it came from the leader of the infidels, and yet there was more to it than that.

Rowan was used to odd feelings. They came, people kept telling her, with being a woman. But this one was odder than she knew what to do with. She started to melt back among the princesses.

Something made her stop. Her father still had not touched the Talisman with his bare hands. He folded it in its wrapping and tucked it into his sleeve, almost as if he had forgotten about it, except that he remembered to thank the Caliph and the Caliph's man with proper courtesy. But that was not what held Rowan still.

The Elephant had stood quietly through the last of

the gift-giving. Suddenly it moved, stretching out its long strange snout as if looking for something. One of its handlers rapped the end with a stick. That must have hurt. The Elephant curled its trunk under its chin and flattened its ears. It was not submitting, though maybe its handlers thought so. The eye that Rowan could see was wise and sad, and said as clearly as words, that the Elephant bided its time.

"They say it will live three hundred years," Rowan said to her mother.

Her mother was dead, which made it easier to talk to her, because one could do it anywhere, but harder too, because then one had to explain what one was doing. Which was why Rowan was kneeling in the little chapel beside the women's hall, her head bowed devoutly over her folded hands and her voice lowered to a mumble. The stone floor was hard under her knees. She could hear her sisters and their ladies chattering in the hall, sounding like a flock of magpies.

"It is the most amazing thing," Rowan went on. Sometimes she liked to imagine that the wooden Virgin beside the altar was her mother. Her mother had been beautiful like that, but never so mild. "It looked so sad, and so wise. I wonder what it was thinking?"

Probably it was homesick, said the voice in Rowan's head that might be her own, but then again might be her mother's. It was something, that was all she knew, that felt like a woman, with a woman's solid common sense, but warmth too, and something that felt like affection.

She could not see any shape to go with it, either spirit-form or earthly flesh. But whatever it was, it knew about homesickness. Heaven was all very well, but one missed one's kin.

"*I* shouldn't miss them," Rowan said with sudden temper. "I should like to go as far away as the moon. Then I wouldn't have to listen to Rothaide. She was at me this morning again, about how she might be a concubine's daughter, but I'm born of a witch. She said that, Mother, right to my face. I hit her. It wasn't womanly, I know it wasn't. Men are the ones who do all the hitting. But I had to do it. Rothaide is always saying dreadful things about everybody, but she isn't going to say them about you."

And what if what Rothaide said was true?

Rowan forgot to keep her head down. She glared at the gentle somber Virgin who after all looked nothing like her fierce gold-and-white mother. "You were not a witch! You were a queen. You didn't let people forget that. Some of them don't forgive."

Including Rothaide, the concubine's child. Bitter, beautiful Rothaide, with her terrible tongue.

"Oh," said Rowan, letting her head droop forward again. She was not going to weep. She had given up weeping. But her throat was tight. "Mother, I wish you hadn't died. *You* would know why I'm in such a tangle. You wouldn't smile the way the others do, and nod, and talk oh so wisely about how a child becomes a woman. I don't want to be a child. I don't want to be a woman either, or a princess. I want to be just Rowan."

And was Rowan not Rowan already?

"I mean all the time," said Rowan. "Not just when I'm riding my pony or talking to you."

But everyone had to be more than one's simple self. Particularly if one was a princess, and meant for the great things of the world.

"If Father would ever let any of us out of his sight," said Rowan. "He keeps us like birds in an aviary. We can have anything we want, do anything we please—except fly away."

And did she want to?

Rowan stood up. Her knees were stiff. The women were quieter now: one of them was telling a story. Rowan loved stories, but not today. Not with a whole live Elephant to think of.

She was running away from her mother's relentless good sense, she knew that very well. But some things she was not ready to face.

She remembered to cross herself, in case anyone was looking. No one was. She tucked up her skirts and made sure her braids were wound tight about her head and her veil secure over them, and set off toward the stable.

Two

WELL BEFORE Rowan came to the stable, she heard what sounded like a battle in full cry, complete with trumpets. She hitched up her skirts and ran.

There were no horses in the battle, at least. But there were men enough in the next courtyard over from the stable, and boys with them, and in the middle the Elephant. The great beast was holding them all off with trunk and tusks and short charges. There were ropes on it, but they swung loose or dangled broken. No one dared to run in close enough to seize a trailing end.

As far as Rowan could tell, the men wanted to shut the Elephant in the pavilion that had been set up for it until they could build it a house in the Emperor's menagerie. The pavilion was one of the Emperor's old war-tents with three sides down and one rolled up, and the Elephant wanted no part of it.

Rowan knew she should slip round the other way and do something that would explain her presence here, such as get her pony saddled and led out to ride. But she stayed where she was, backed against the wall.

One of the grooms had taken the same refuge from the battle. He cradled a bruised hand, and he cursed the Elephant under his breath, till he sensed Rowan's eyes on him. Then he blushed and shut his mouth.

"Hasn't it ever seen a tent before?" Rowan asked.

"God knows," said the groom. "These monsters have their own keepers, the infidels say. Raised with them, sleep with them, feed them and clean them and for all I know make water with them. This one's keeper died of a fever somewhere south of Cologne. It's been barely manageable ever since."

"Poor thing," said Rowan. She got a grip on the boy's hand before he could muster wits to stop her. "Not broken," she said, and never mind his yelp when she flexed his fingers. "Wrap it in a cold poultice and don't use it too much for a while."

She let him go. He hugged his hand as if it had been a wounded baby, and glowered.

"It's in mourning," Rowan said, watching the Elephant's fight. "No wonder it doesn't want to do what everyone's asking. Didn't anybody think to ask it quietly?"

Certainly the groom had not. Rowan was about to step into the fray herself, with no particular idea of what she would do when she got there, when someone walked out of the yelling crowd and into the circle the Elephant had cleared. The yelling changed focus. "You young fool! Do you want it to trample you?"

The young fool paid no attention. He was Rowan's age, probably, not quite a boy, not quite a man, slight and dark, in dusty plain clothes. He walked as calmly as if he were going out to the pasture of a morning to fetch a meek old pony. He had a knot of grass in his hand, too, fresh and green, and where he had got that in the middle of Aachen, Rowan could not imagine.

The noise was deafening, and probably had something to do with the Elephant's rage. Rowan could not hear what the boy said, but she saw his lips move. He was talking to the beast as if it could hear, let alone understand.

The Elephant stood still. Its trunk was up, threatening, but it did not charge. It would let the boy get in close, Rowan could tell. Then it would crush him.

Rowan bit down on the back of her hand. No one was making any move to distract the Elephant or to rescue the boy. She took off her veil. It was not much, but if she flapped it in the Elephant's face—

She got as far as the edge of the crowd before she realized what was happening. The boy had his hand on the Elephant's shoulder, stroking it. The Elephant shuddered. Now it would move. Now it would trample him.

Its trunk came down. Rowan poised to leap.

As gently as a lady plucking a May blossom, the pink tip of the trunk curled round the end of the grass-twist. The boy let the twist go. The Elephant tucked it into the mouth that hid under the trunk and the tusks, and chewed slowly, solemnly.

There was no sound but that, and the breathing of too many people pressed too close, and the boy's soft voice speaking in a strange language. For a moment Rowan thought he was an infidel. He was dark enough for one, and his nose was a fierce enough curve. But he did not feel to her like one of the Caliph's men, of whom there were many in the yard, and he was not dressed like them, either. His tunic was Frankish without a doubt, and his shaggy head was bare of a turban.

He stroked the Elephant and talked to it, while everyone stared. After a while he seemed to notice that he was not alone in the world. He said in clear Frankish with a hint of a lilt, "You may go away now. Abul Abbas is tired of your noise. He says that he will go into his prison, if only he may rest there in peace."

Rowan found that her mouth was open. She shut it. She was a princess of the Franks, and she had seen a fair lot of arrogant young lordlings. She had never seen anything to match this stableboy in the dusty tunic.

More startling still, people obeyed him. The Caliph's men bowed in the way they had, touching brow and lip and breast. Her father's people were louder and less orderly, but even they did as the boy told them. The few who stayed clearly had business to keep them there.

The boy seemed to have forgotten them again. He took the Elephant's trunk as if it had been a child's hand, and led the great beast into the tent.

It was dim under the sag of the roof, with an odor of old canvas, and something indescribable that must have been the Elephant. There was hay laid out, enough to fill a cart, and water in a barrel, and a bed of good straw. The Elephant tasted the hay, using its trunk like a hand,

and drank from the barrel in a way that made Rowan gape: drawing up a trunkful of water and sucking it into its mouth. She would have been horrified if it had not been so interesting.

She stayed near the open side of the tent, for prudence, although the Elephant seemed quiet now. It looked at her once or twice, without any hostility that she could see. She did not know whether she found that comforting. Now that she understood its sadness, she had a powerful temptation to go to it and put her arms around it and tell it that she understood. Her mother had died when she was young, and her nurse when she was a little older. She knew what it was to lose something that one loved.

If she did not go soon, it would be dark before she could saddle her pony and ride. The shadows were long in the yard. The Elephant was hardly more than a shape and a gleam of gold-tipped tusks. But she stayed where she was.

The boy's shadow moved apart from the Elephant's. His voice was sharp. "Didn't I tell you to go away?"

"Why should I have listened?" Rowan asked him. She had been studying Gisela; she knew how to make her voice perfectly, maddeningly sweet.

"You're upsetting Abul Abbas," the boy said.

The Elephant was not upset. He was paying them no attention at all. Rowan decided to follow his example, and ignore the boy's nonsense. "Is that his name? Abul-labas?"

"Abul Abbas." The boy's precision was insulting.

"My name is Theoderada," said Rowan, "but everyone calls me Rowan. Father Angilbert gave us all poetry-names, you see, when we were little. Gisela is Lily, Bertha is Rose, Hrotrud is Linden—"

"Theoderada is Chatterbox." The boy was sneering, she could tell, even if it was too dark to see.

"And what," asked Rowan, "do they call you?"

She did not think that he would answer, but after a while he did, biting it off short. "Kerrec."

"Kerrec," said Rowan, "and Abul Abbas." She took care to say it correctly. "How is it that you know about elephants?"

That, he did not reply to.

"I suppose you'll be his keeper now," she said, "since no one else can manage him. It will make a change from horses."

"Will you just," he said tightly, "go away? So that Abul Abbas can rest?"

Really, thought Rowan, he was rude beyond words, even if he was too much a stranger to know who she was. She was not in a mood to enlighten him, but neither was she so contrary as to argue with the dismissal. The Elephant had fought a hard battle. He would be tired, and he would want to do his grieving in solitude. Though maybe the grief would be less now, with Kerrec to keep him company. Rowan would have hated it, but she could see what kind of person Kerrec was: no time or sympathy for people, but a world of it for animals.

She had just enough time to saddle her pony and to manage a canter round the knights' field, which was empty for once, except for a hen that had wandered in from somewhere. The bird was too haughty or too stupid to care that it was in Galla's way, and Galla made do, when necessary, by jumping neatly over it. It would have been better sport if they could have taken longer at it, and if the flies had not come to the feast. Galla's warding of watered vinegar was wearing thin. When the pony flew into a bucking fit round the whole rim of the field, Rowan brought her in.

Rowan liked to do her own stablehanding, even the stalls when there was no one near to be scandalized. Tonight the grooms were all either huddled in corners talking about the Elephant or absorbed in looking after the embassy's beautiful little horses. Galla was half Arab herself, and it showed in her fine head and her elegant tail, but she had enough good Frankish cob in her to make her sensible.

Rowan brushed the red-brown coat till it shone, and sponged on another bowlful of vinegar. Galla snorted at it, but it kept the flies at bay. A bit of bread mollified her, and a fistful of dried apple.

It was dark by the time Rowan left the stable. There were lamps lit in the yard, and one by the Elephant's pavilion. She heard Abul Abbas moving about inside, but she did not go back to see him and certainly not to see his keeper. "Good night, Lord Elephant," she said softly. Maybe he paused, listening. Maybe he was only comfortable at last, and slipping into sleep.

Three

· · · · · · · · · · · · ·

*T*HE CALIPH'S MEN stayed through spring into summer, feasting and hunting and talking politics. In the middle of that, more people came, dark bearded men from the east like the Caliph's men, but these were Christians, and they spoke Greek, and called themselves servants of the Empress of the East. They hated the Caliph's men. The Caliph's men hated them. They were all excruciatingly polite, because Rowan's father was stronger than any of them.

The palace was bursting at the seams. The women had to double up in the little rooms behind their hall. They were sleeping crammed together like sheep in a pen, and falling over one another in the daytime, trying to stay out of the way of all the embassies.

The little chapel where Rowan went to talk to her mother was full of sloe-eyed bearded priests. The stable was full of foreign horses—Galla was put out to pasture, and never mind what Rowan thought of that. There was no place to go to be by herself, except maybe one.

She made an excuse, to begin with. She really was

out of thread for the border she was embroidering, or trying to embroider when she had to stop every few stitches to let someone climb over her.

She knew perfectly well that she should find a maid to run the errand, or ask one of her sisters to go with her. But that had always been her chief rebellion: to go out alone. There was silver in her purse, and a fistful of copper. It would do. She put on her plainest gown and tied up her hair in a bit of linen. Her heart was racing, which was silly. She went alone to the market all the time. But it never quite stopped being an adventure.

With the Caliph's men in the city, and now the Byzantines, the market had swelled out of its square and into the streets round about. Merchants came from everywhere to show their wares, and people came to buy them or to trade for them. Cooks and bakers came in to feed the crowds, and sellers of wine and ale, and butchers and poulterers, cheesemongers, spice-merchants, greengrocers and fruitsellers; and for those who ate too much, apothecaries with their stalls full of wonderful things. Rowan could follow her nose through the market, pork roasting here, cheese aging there, bread baking, wine spilling, and once a sweetness so strong that she staggered: spices whose names she barely knew, steeped in honey and mixed in cakes or wine.

She was not looking for things to eat. Simply smelling them was enough. In among them she found the other things: gold and silver and copper, bronze and iron forged into shapes as noble as weapons or as lowly as buckles for a harness, perfumes as powerful as the spices, flowers as potent as the perfumes, the good pungent smell of well-tanned leather, the warm oily scent of woven wool, the dusty-dry smell of linen.

She found the thread she was looking for, woven gold and dear enough to all but empty her purse, but the woman who sold it to her slipped in a twist of silk, too. "To match your eyes," she said. The silk was an odd color, which was probably why it came unpaid for: not quite grey, not quite green. Rowan liked to think that her eyes were greyer than that, or at least less muddy. They would not ever be pure clear blue like Bertha's or Gisela's. Her hair was no-color, too, beside Bertha's wheat-gold and Gisela's wonderful almost-silver: neither brown nor gold but somewhere between.

She was glad of the thread, for all that, and she said so. The way the woman looked at her, Rowan knew her name was no secret, or her rank, either. But people in the Emperor's city had a courtesy. They let the Emperor's children go unnoticed if they wanted it.

With her booty in her purse next to a lonely copper penny, Rowan took the long way back to the palace. She skirted the walls and meandered for a while through the narrow twisting streets, now up toward the great tall tower that was her father's chapel, now down round the crumbling Roman pillars of the baths. There was a garden in back of that. The gate had a latch and a bolt, but it opened when she tried it. She slipped through.

Her father's garden was young yet. There were trees

that would be lovely when they were older, and beds of flowers that needed to thicken a little, like hair on a baby's head. But the little orchard that had been there since the palace was a Roman villa, was thriving handsomely. Rowan could feel the cool of the trees even before she came to them, blessed in the day's heat. There were bees singing in the grass, and a flock of sparrows squabbling in the branches.

Her favorite tree stood in the middle. It was ancient but sturdy, and it bore a good crop every year. The best of it, aside from its apples, was the way it branched, making a seat just the right size for Rowan. If she rested her back against the rise of the trunk and stretched her legs along the twining of two branches, only someone who knew where to look could see her from below. She had eluded nurses so when she was small, and officious callers-to-duty when she was bigger.

She clambered up to her seat. It was cooler there than it was below, with a bit of a breeze. She opened her bodice to let the breeze in, and tucked her skirts above her knees, and grinned at the pattern of leaves above her. Scandalous, simply scandalous.

She did not mean to stay long, but the sun was warm through the leaves, and the bees sang of sleep. Her eyelids drooped.

Voices startled her awake. They were not loud, but they were right below her. She caught herself before she could roll off her perch, and peered cautiously down.

They sat on the grass at the tree's foot: a woman in

a veil confined by a thin fillet only a little more silver than her hair, and a man with hair as blackly curly as a lapdog's coat. He had a curly beard, too, and a soft wheedling voice. Rowan would have known what he was even without his elaborate coat. There was no mistaking the sound of a Byzantine in full slither.

What was shocking was that he was slithering about sick-sweet saintly Gisela instead of somebody hotterblooded, like Rothaide. Gisela fended him off, but feebly.

"Such beauty," said the Byzantine in accented Latin. "A flower among the Franks. And you say that you wish to wed God and not a man. Surely God never meant you to wither away in a cold cloister."

"God is a jealous husband," said Gisela, "and my father is worse. He says that I may go to the convent— but not now, never now, always later. He loves his daughters, you see. He won't let any of us go anywhere that isn't with him. Not to marry, not to serve God, not to do anything but be beautiful for him, and—I shouldn't say it, but I can't lie, either, that's a sin—be perfectly, dreadfully bored."

"Surely," said the Byzantine, "one need not pray only in a convent. One can pray anywhere that one is."

"It's not the same," said Gisela.

"That may be," said the Byzantine. "And does he keep you with him even in his wars?"

"Oh," said Gisela. "Oh, no! He'd never do that."

The Byzantine laughed. "So maidenly an outrage! And so charming. How did we fail to hear of you even in our fair City? You should be a wonder of the world."

That was too much even for Gisela. "Really," she

said in a tone that, in anyone else, would have been waspish. "You don't need to flatter me to death. You're very nice to look at. I like the way you sing. Won't you sing me the song you promised, that you learned only for me?"

"Of course," he said. His long fingers had, one way and another, got rid of her veil. He started on the pins that held her braids. First one fell to her shoulders, then another. Then he loosened the heavy plaits, working them free of the ribbons that bound them. Gisela never moved. Either he had her under a spell, or she had decided that he was not dangerous.

Gisela had always been an idiot. Rowan thought of arranging to fall out of the tree, but matters had not gone far enough for that. Yet.

At first Rowan did not realize that the Byzantine was singing. He sang softly, like the humming of bees and the sighing of wind in the leaves. The words were in Greek, of which Rowan knew a little. They told her nothing, except that one of them was *love*. Gisela sat as still as the tree, with her hair a silvery shimmer about her. Even from above she was astonishingly beautiful.

The song slid seamlessly into speech. "As lovely as you are," he said, "only the most wonderful of jewels is worthy of you. Would that I were a king or a mighty mage, to lay the wealth of the world at your feet."

"I have all that I need," Gisela said.

"So fair a saint!" the Byzantine marveled. "And what if you chose but one jewel of all that are, one that itself is holy?"

Gisela's hand went to her breast where lay her golden

cross. "I have it here," she said, "in the sweet Christ's name."

"Would you have another more holy yet?"

"There is no such thing," Gisela said.

"Oh," he said, "but there is."

She must have widened her eyes. He tilted his head so that Rowan could see his smile, sweet and cloying. "There is one jewel," he said, "of which you alone are worthy, to which you alone should be entitled. Unbelievers brought it from the East, from the Caliph of the infidels, but it is a purely Christian thing."

Rowan's fingers locked on the branch beside her.

"A small thing," he said, "a precious thing, a golden Talisman. A relic of the True Cross set in gold and crystal, wrought to hang about an empress' neck."

"And where would I find such a thing?" Gisela asked.

"Where indeed?" said the Byzantine. "Is not your father the greatest of kings in the West? And is he not the boon companion of the infidel Caliph?"

"They've brought him a whole kingdom's worth of gifts," said Gisela. "Even an elephant. But I haven't seen a relic of the True Cross."

"Indeed," the Byzantine said. "He received it quietly and hid it away quickly. He knows that it is not for him. If you should approach him, ask him for the gift that is your right . . ."

"But is it?" Gisela sat up straighter, and her voice was almost sharp. "Why would I want it, if my father has it?"

"For your beauty's sake," the Byzantine answered

promptly, "and for your soul's protection. It is a holy thing, this Talisman, and a strong one. Who knows? With it in your hands, you might succeed at last in persuading your father to let you go into your cloister."

"Magic," said Gisela. "You're talking about magic."

"I am talking about a blessed relic, wood of the Tree on which Our Savior died." He crossed himself devoutly, backwards, in the Byzantine fashion. "Your father thinks nothing of it. He keeps it locked away with the rest of his unconsidered treasures, gifts he has received but can make no use of, riches so profuse that they have ceased to matter at all. Why should the favorite of his daughters be lacking her soul's protection and her heart's desire, because he is not even aware that he has it?"

"And what do you know of my heart's desire?"

Shrewd, that question, and it took the Byzantine aback. Rowan could have told him that Gisela was like that. She never saw what was plain to see, except when she was not supposed to see it.

He recovered quickly. "I can't tell you that," he said with purely mendacious candor. "A vow, the honor of a friend and kinsman . . . but there, I say too much. Do you wonder at all that this most Christian of relics should come to you from the hands of an infidel? It never began there. It will not, please God, end there."

"It's yours?" Gisela asked almost eagerly. "You want it back?"

"Oh, no! It's never mine. If anyone has right to it, it is you. It was given to your father. It was made to protect a pure soul from the snares of temptation. He, may he

23

live forever, is a mighty king, but purity of soul he has never had. You, on the other hand . . ."

"I'm a terrible sinner," said Gisela. "Do you really think I deserve this relic?"

"More than any other," the Byzantine said with fervor that rang suspiciously true.

"I don't know," Gisela said. "It seems like vanity, somehow."

Rowan could almost hear the Byzantine's teeth grinding. "Is it vanity to say a Paternoster? 'And lead us not into temptation, but deliver us from evil.' That is what this relic is. A prayer set in gold, with the wood of the Tree in its heart."

Gisela clasped her hands to her breast. "Oh, yes. Yes, if you put it that way. It's not vanity at all; it's almost a sin to refuse."

"So it is," the Byzantine said. He did not quite manage to keep the satisfaction out of his tone.

"I'll ask my father tonight," said Gisela. "He'll give it to me. He gives me anything I ask for."

"Except what you desire most," said the Byzantine.

"And with the relic, I'll pray that he may give me leave to go into the cloister." Gisela stood up, taking no notice of the hair that tumbled down her back. "Oh, how I'll pray for that!"

Four

*A*FTER GISELA WENT AWAY, the Byzantine lingered till Rowan nearly flung herself out of the tree to end the suspense. But he never looked up. He smiled to himself and said something in Greek. Rowan was not sure she wanted to know what. She was remembering what people said about Byzantines. They were all sorcerers, and their Empress was the greatest sorceress of them all. And if one of them wanted a certain Talisman, a relic of the True Cross . . .

The Byzantine left still smiling. Rowan clung to her branch and shook. It was a long while before she was steady enough to climb down.

Once she was on the grass, her knees would barely hold her up. She sat for a while and tried to breathe. "I can't help it," she said to the air, or maybe to her mother. "He probably means nothing. He wants a look at the Caliph's gift, that's all, or he honestly thinks Gisela should have it. Who knows how his people think? But I can't—I just can't—like a Byzantine. Or ever, ever trust one."

No one in the world could. Everybody hated the Byzantines. That was why they were so powerful.

"That and magic," Rowan said.

Maybe.

She made herself stand up.

It was easier once she started walking. Her feet led her through the stable, to the one part of it that was quiet. The part that housed the Elephant.

Everywhere else was humming. Where the Elephant was, there was no one, and no sound but the buzzing of flies and the soft enormous roar of the Elephant's breathing. The Elephant seemed to be asleep. His keeper was nowhere that Rowan could see. She was glad.

The Elephant woke when she wavered on the edge of his tent, under the rolled-up awning. It was nothing very obvious; she simply knew that he was aware of her. She was not afraid. Fear was somewhere behind her.

The wise sad eye seemed to beckon. She approached slowly, ready to bolt if he made a move, but he only watched her. She found herself right in front of him, close enough to touch. His skin looked rough, almost scaly, but it was soft, wrinkled like a very old woman's, and warm. His trunk moved very slowly as if to assure her that it meant no harm, circling around her. It felt like a strong warm arm. The great foreleg lifted in front of her. It looked like the step of a stair. His eye seemed to smile. She set her foot on the Elephant's leg, and all at once the trunk was around her like a strong arm and she was rising, up to the place that God had made for a person to sit in: the hollow of the neck behind the broad soft flaps of the ears. She fit there as well as she did in her tree. The great domed head was in front of her, and the great arched back behind. She was higher than she had ever been on a horse.

She tried not to grip too hard and pinch. It was terrifying, but it was wonderful, to sit up here in the lofty shade, staring out at the sunlit world.

It did not quite make her forget why she was here. "They want something, those Byzantines," she said to the Elephant. "And not just the Caliph's Talisman."

But of course, said the voice in her head, which maybe was her mother, or maybe the Elephant, or maybe just her own common sense. The Empress of the East wanted to marry the Emperor of the West. She had sent her embassy to ask it—command it, some people said. The Empress of the East thought she was the ruler of the world and great Carl was just a barbarian, a rough uncivilized nobody who dared to call himself her equal.

"She blinded her own son," Rowan said: "put out his eyes with a hot iron, so that she could be empress. What will she do to Father if she gets her hands on him?"

Carl was stronger than that. Had he not been holding off the terrible Empress for years, and taking the West for himself?

"But," said Rowan, "that was before the Caliph's men came here. Before the Talisman." She hated even to say the word, it troubled her so much. "And I don't know why!" she cried to the hot still air. The Elephant did not move under her, though she could feel him listening: a bit of tension in his neck, a tilt of his ears as if to catch what she said. She patted his head in shaky apology.

"I don't know why," she said more quietly. "I don't

think he even remembers it. I've never seen him wear it. It's in a box somewhere, I suppose, with all the other things people give him because he's the Emperor."

That would be like him, the air admitted. Carl never forgot anything that mattered, but little things went right out of his head.

"That Talisman isn't a little thing," Rowan said. "It only looks like one."

Maybe, the air suggested, Rowan was only jealous because her father was thinking about marrying again, but he would let none of his daughters have a husband— because, he said, he loved them too much to let them go.

"What? Jealous of *her?*" Rowan almost laughed. "I'd rather be jealous of mating snakes. Although," she said, "I do wish . . ."

That she could marry?

"Someday," she said, "I'm going to. I promised myself. I'm going to be ordinary. I'm going to be happy. Happy is a house that's mine, a man who's mine, children—everything that a simple woman can have. Maybe I'll work myself to the bone. Father says women like that do. Maybe I'll be old and grey and toothless when I'm no older than Bertha. But I'll be happy."

She looked down. It was a very long way to the ground. She shut her eyes, took a deep breath, and started sliding.

Something stopped her. She opened her eyes. The Elephant's leg was lifted again, making its stair. She stepped down the last bit and put her arms around his trunk, and hugged carefully. He hugged back. She smiled.

Her eyes were watery, God knew why. "Thank you," she said.

"For what?"

Rowan spun like a cat.

The Elephant's boy looked furious. "What are you doing? Get away from my Elephant!"

"*Your* Elephant?" Rowan came down off terror into pure rage. "And just who do you think you are?"

That stopped him.

"This is the Emperor's Elephant," Rowan said. "I am the Emperor's daughter. Therefore—"

"What is this, a schoolroom?" Kerrec—Rowan would not have condescended to remember his name, but her memory was being fickle—Kerrec seemed to be able to stay in control of himself, even when he was in a temper. And he had not even blinked, let alone flinched, when she flung her rank in his face. It was all intensely annoying. "You could have been hurt."

"My lord Abul Abbas would never hurt me," Rowan said. She was not going to tell Kerrec that she had ridden the Elephant; or at least sat on him. That would give the boy proper fits.

He snorted like one of the horses. "All you princesses are alike. Nothing in the world can touch you, because you're who you are. Haven't you ever heard what happens to pride that goes too far?"

"In Scripture," said Rowan with just enough edge to be nasty, "it falls. In the Romans' books it makes the gods jealous. In Greece—"

He muttered something.

"What language is that?" she asked him.

He looked startled. Good. Men could never think of more than one thing at once: it gave them a headache. He blurted the answer before he could have thought. "Breton."

"You're from Brittany?" That explained much, including his dark hawkish looks and his dreadful manners. "That was Count Roland's country. He died years before I was born, but everyone remembers him."

Kerrec went stiff. For a moment Rowan thought he was going to hit her. His hands were knotted into fists, and his face looked like a fist itself, clenched tight.

Rowan kept talking. Babbling, really, but if she stopped, she did not know what would happen. "If you're a Breton, you know about magic, yes? Brittany has magic in its bones. But not the kind of magic that's in the East, so maybe it's not going to help. What the infidels have— what's in Byzantium—"

"What do you know of Byzantium?"

Rowan's teeth clicked together. This was absolute idiocy, but it kept coming out of her. The whole thing. The garden, Gisela, the Byzantine with his soft voice and his slithery ways.

It was Kerrec's face, she decided while her tongue went on. It was a thoroughly dislikable face, but not the way the Byzantine's was. That face made her want to hold tight to every secret. This one made her want to pry it open and let the light in, gather up the dry tinder that was inside and set it afire.

And anyway, Kerrec was nobody. A stableboy who

looked after an elephant. The Elephant. Who trusted him, and who talked to him, maybe told him stories in the nights, wonderful tales from places beyond the moon.

The words ran dry. Rowan stood blinking. She was sickening for something, maybe. She felt dizzy, as if she had a touch of fever.

Kerrec did not tell her that she was out of her head. She wished he would. He did not say anything for so long that she decided he was not going to, and moved to push past him.

He caught her arm. She stared at his hand. His dark cheeks flushed; he let go. "Why did you tell me this?" he asked her.

"I don't know," she said.

"Because you're the witch's daughter?"

She was too tired to hit him. "She wasn't a witch."

"I think maybe she wasn't," he said, "after all. But you—"

"I'm not. I don't have any magic in me at all."

"You don't know—" He stopped. "No, you don't. What do they teach you here?"

"Grammar," said Rowan. "Rhetoric. Logic. Music, astronomy, geometry, arithmetic. Latin, a tiny bit of Greek, a little Arabic. Poetry, philosophy, theology—"

"Nothing," he said. "Not a thing that you need to know."

"And I suppose you know everything?"

"I know about magic." He said it remarkably calmly. "We do know about that, in Brittany."

He was mocking her, but not enough to make her

angry. "You're not a stableboy, are you?" she said in realization that was not quite sudden; it had been growing for a while. "You don't talk like one. You understand everything I tell you—empresses and caliphs and schools and all the rest of it. They don't teach such things between the hayloft and the stalls."

"Unless you mean monks' stalls." That was a flash of humor, so quick she wondered if she had seen it at all. "No, I'm not that, either. I didn't run away from a monastery."

Rowan stared at him. For once she was empty of words.

"Don't let your sister get that Talisman," he said, looking like himself again, dark and sulky and damnably arrogant.

Everything in her said that he was right, but the way he said it, as if he had a right to order her about, made her go all contrary. "And why shouldn't she, after all? What can she do with it? It's just a pretty relic. She loves relics, especially when they've jewels on them."

His expression was pure male exasperation. "What she can do with it doesn't matter in the least. It's what Michael Phokias will do when she lets him touch it."

"Is that his name? I never noticed. No, he shouldn't get it. But who says Gisela will give it to him?"

"You do!" He threw up his hands. "Why do I bother with any of this? Let her take the thing. Let her give it to him. Then see what he does with it. What should I care? This house could fall about my ears, and I'd be no worse off than I've ever been."

"Are you laying a curse on my father's house?" Rowan asked, low and very calm.

"I don't need to. The Byzantine will do it for me."

She hit him. Not the way a lady would, a weak flat-handed slap, but a good solid blow of the fist in the face, sweeping him right off his feet. He went down in blank astonishment. She stood over him. He stared up, rubbing his jaw. "You'll have a bruise," she observed.

"You're moon-mad," he said.

"Of course I am. I'm a woman."

He lay in the hay with his jaw already going purple, and he laughed. It was dreadfully catching. Rowan's knees gave out. She toppled beside him, holding her aching sides.

She blinked through tears of laughter. Kerrec looked no better blurred than clear. "Tell me," she said, "why a Byzantine should want to get hold of a single relic in a whole palace full of them."

"I don't know," he said. Then when she glared: "This isn't just a relic. You know that as well as I do, or you wouldn't be here, running out on what you very well know you should be doing."

"What? Embroidering crosses on an altar cloth?"

He did not dignify that with a response. "Have you wondered why he doesn't just steal it?"

"He's a Byzantine. Byzantines can never do anything the simple way."

"Granted; and seducing your saintly sister would be just the sort of thing to spice the game. But," said Kerrec, "what if there's a reason why it's not to be stolen— why it has to be a free gift?"

"A spell?" Rowan asked.

"How did you feel when you saw it?"

She shivered.

"You see," he said. "Your eyes get all white around the edges when you talk about it. And you didn't even touch it. Or did you?"

"No," she said. "Oh, no."

"I think," said Kerrec. "I'm not sure, but I think . . . there's something the Talisman is meant to do."

"Something bad?" Rowan whispered, huddling in on herself.

"Do you think so?"

She did not want to think at all, but his eyes were so steady that she could not help it. After a while she said slowly, "No. I don't think it's bad. Just . . . strong. And—wild?"

"Unmastered," said Kerrec.

Rowan sat up so quickly her head spun. "You've seen it!"

"No," said Kerrec. He was not looking at her. She twisted about. The Elephant stood as he always did, but something about him made her think that he listened.

"Abul Abbas knows," said Kerrec. "He isn't telling. He says we aren't ready."

"You really *can* talk to him," Rowan said. After everything else, it was hardly worth remarking on.

"He says," said Kerrec, "that you have to make your father keep the jewel. Make him wear it, if you can."

"Why?"

Kerrec's brows drew together. He looked as if he was

getting a headache. "It's not for your sister, and not—ever—for your father's enemies."

"Will it destroy them, do you think?" Rowan asked hopefully. "Blast them when they touch it?"

"If it were that easy," said Kerrec, "do you think we'd have to do anything about it?"

"I don't know," said Rowan. "It's all impossible. You're making it up. I'm making it up. It's just a splinter in a crystal, and that's just an elephant, and you're just a stableboy. And I—I'm just Rowan. I don't want to be anything else."

"Do you think God cares what you want?"

"I think," said Rowan, "that you are appalling." She scrambled up, shaking hay from her skirt. There was hay in her hair, too. She brushed at it. Her hands shook. "You'll hold your tongue, or I'll have it cut out."

That anyone could look as if he had drawn himself to a full and impressive height while lying flat in a pile of hay, Rowan would not have believed till she saw it. He got up with more grace than she had, and bowed so perfectly that it was like a slap. "As her highness wishes," said the Elephant's boy.

Five

IT WAS TOO LATE to stop Gisela.

She must have waylaid the Emperor when he came from the baths. He was always expansive then, flushed with warm water and good exercise, smelling of sweet herbs and clean wool, and ready for a long evening's feasting and talking. All his daughters knew that that was the best time to wheedle a favor out of him, when he knew perfectly well what they were doing, but was too delighted with himself and his world to refuse.

By the time Rowan found him, he was in the women's hall surrounded by his daughters and their ladies, and Gisela was leaning on his shoulder. She had always been his favorite, his white lily. He had his arm around her, and he was smiling while she murmured in his ear.

The rest went about what they were doing. Most of them were working on embroidery. Bertha was reading from a book—something Latin, and sonorous. Rowan wanted to scream at them all, wake them up, set them on their traitorous, innocent sister.

She could not even pass the doorway. Sunlight through

a high window cast a ray of light on the two in the room's center, turned the Emperor's hair to ruddy gold and Gisela's to shining silver. They looked like painted saints. Even his voice did not break the moment. It was as high as always, but sweet to listen to, warm and indulgent. "Of course you may have it. It's too pretty for me, but you'll look a right beauty in it."

"Then," Gisela said, cooing soft like a dove, "may I have it now, do you think—if it's not asking too much—?"

He laughed. "Of course you may have it now. I'll send Odo with it; then you can wear it at dinner. Wear your best dress, too, the blue silk that suits you so well, and we'll show the princes of the East what beauty we have here in the barbarous West."

Gisela blushed and simpered. Rowan ground her teeth.

She had not lost yet. The Emperor had to walk by her as he went out. First he kissed each of his daughters and said polite things to their ladies, and made a great show of reluctance to leave them. Not that it was false; he did love his daughters' company. But he was not a man to sit still for long.

He did not start when he saw Rowan, or object when she fell in beside him, trotting to keep up with his long strides. "Get thrown in a hayrick, did you?" he said.

Rowan's cheeks were hot. He kept his face stern, but his eyes glinted. He reached out, plucked a stem from above her ear, inspected it as he strode on. "New crop," he observed.

They rounded a corner. One more passage and they would be in his own rooms amid crowds of people. Here there was no one. The servants would be in the hall, getting it ready for dinner. The guests were all out hunting or prowling or keeping one another company.

Rowan caught hold of her father's sleeve and dug in her heels. He came to a halt. "Father," she said, "don't give Gisela the Talisman."

His brows went up. He was not angry. He never lost his temper with his children unless they gave him strong cause. Nor had she surprised him. "So you heard that, did you? You'll all be getting something. I thought you might be more partial to one of the infidels' horses. There's one, the bay with the white foot—"

Oh, that was temptation, but Rowan was not to be distracted. "I don't want the thing. I just don't want you to give it to Gisela."

"Jealousy's a sin, you know," her father said.

Rowan stamped her foot. "I'm not jealous! I just—"

"You don't want me to give the relic to Gisela. Why? It's very much her sort of bauble. She'll take better care of it than anyone else would. Even," he said, "you."

He was laughing at her. And she was forgetting that she was a woman now: she heard her voice spiral up to a whine. "Father! The Caliph gave it to *you*."

"And he'll be delighted to know that I thought enough of it to give it to my daughter."

"Your favorite daughter." Rowan did not mind that. Gisela was an idiot, but she was the kind of idiot people could not help but be fond of. "She's not going to keep it, Father. She's going to give it to—somebody."

Her voice caught on the name. She bit her tongue trying to say it, or anything that would tell her father enough to make him listen.

The Emperor did not seem to notice. "I'll tell her not to give it away," he said.

"You shouldn't give it away at all," said Rowan.

For a moment she thought she had him. He actually looked as if he was listening; now, please God, he would ask her why she was so insistent, and please God she would be able to explain.

The moment fled. Somebody called his name, an echo down a stair. He smiled, dropped a kiss on her forehead, and was gone. She would have had to run to catch him.

And for what? To tell him that the Elephant had warned her not to let him do this? That a Byzantine had tempted Gisela—he might have listened to that, but then he would have laughed at the thought of Gisela tempted by anything but a veil and a cloister.

Rowan wished she really were a witch's child. Then she would know spells and wishings, and ways to make the blind see.

But she was only Rowan. She had wanted to be that. Wanting and being, she was beginning to think, were not at all alike.

Gisela had the Talisman. She wore it to dinner with her best gown, the blue silk from Byzantium that made her look more silvery-fair than ever. The relic glowed on her breast, gold and crystal and the bright droplets of jewels.

And nothing happened. No lightnings leaped out of

the golden rondel. No devil came to take it, Byzantine or otherwise. It hung on its chain like any other jewel, larger than most and stranger, but no shudder of magic in it.

It was all foolishness. As for Kerrec, with all his frets and fears—he was the worst fool of all. Talking with the Elephant, of all things. Even Rowan knew better than to believe that.

For a month and more, the quiet went on: long slow dreaming days and brief warm nights. On the eve of Midsummer Rowan went back to the orchard, daring herself to do it, but the only company she had there was a flock of sparrows.

The Caliph's men went back to their own country. The Byzantines stayed, but Rowan kept out of their way. She kept watch on Gisela. As far as she ever saw, Gisela did not meet with the Byzantine named Michael Phokias, nor with any other man.

On a night so warm and still that even the moon seemed to be asleep, Rowan crept out of her bed in the women's hall. She had her own room back again at last, and it had a window that opened on the courtyard, but there was no air in it. She stepped softly over Bertrada, the maid who shared the room. Bertrada did not even pause in her snoring.

It was pitch dark in the passage, but Rowan knew her way. The stair caught her before she was ready. She stumbled, then steadied herself, picking her way down, watchful of the creak in the seventh step. The door at the bottom was latched but not bolted. She opened it just enough to admit a slender girl-body, and slid softly out.

No guard. There never was on this door. It opened near the midden, which was reeking splendidly in the heat, but after that was the wall and a postern gate and a moonlit corner of the garden. The cook's old dog was sleeping near the gate. It raised its head, eyes gleaming, but did not bark. Rowan paused to scratch its mangy ears. It thumped the ground with its tail. "I'll be back in a little while," she said. "Keep watch for me."

The rest of the way was both lighter and sweeter-scented, going down a short steep slope to a wall that was much older than the other. Old Rome had raised these pale stones and these flat red bricks, and carved the capitals on the columns. Old Aachen was inside of them, Aquisgranum of the Romans, dim whispering vaults filled with the lap of water and the stink of sulfur.

In the daytime the baths were full of people. The Emperor was there as often and as long as he could manage, even holding court in the largest of the pools. That was disconcerting for people who had not been warned, foreigners who could not imagine where to look while the Emperor sat naked in the water, or swam back and forth thinking over their petitions.

Now there were only echoes, and moonlight slanting through the louvers in the roof, and the glimmer of water in the pool. The first few times Rowan came alone to the baths at night, a long while ago, she had come with beating heart, terrified that someone would catch her. But no one ever had. If she was missed, people supposed that she had gone out to the privy, or at most to the garden: and that won her a lecture more than once on the mists and demons of the night. But no one ever seemed to suspect the truth.

In winter it was a shivering, teeth-chattering run through the snow-buried garden, and the bliss of warmth in the hottest pool at the end of it. In summer it was a promise of coolness, a long idle paddle in the coldest pool while the lamp burned down and the moon went its round and she thought her thoughts away from the clatter of the palace. She could talk to her mother here, if she was minded. Her mother very likely would not have approved when she was alive; she was the queen, after all, and the queen had appearances to keep up. But now that she was dead, she could come to Rowan as easily in the baths as in the chapel or the garden, and with much less fear of interruption.

A lamp always burned by the keeper's bench. Why it burned there, Rowan had never learned. The keeper did not come at night, nor did anyone else.

Rowan used the lamp to light the one she had brought. It was convenient not to have to fret with flint and steel. The wick caught easily in the still air, flared and sank and settled to a steady flame. The room that had been black dark and white moonlight grew an island of pale-gold lamplight.

"Maybe," Rowan said to her mother, "the lamp is for me: the spirit who comes to bathe in the night."

Her mother said nothing. Rowan smiled, walking fearlessly through capering shadows. She had thought that she would swim in the coldest pool, but impulse turned her toward the largest one, the one that was both warm and cool. She set her lamp on one of the benches—she barely needed it here, with the moon shining in—and slipped out of her gown.

Something moved.

She froze. Mouse, she thought. Cat, maybe, hunting. There were plenty of both in this place.

It was a very large cat, then, or a whole tribe of mice. And it walked on two feet.

Rowan's gown was crumpled on the pool's rim. She shivered in her shift. Stupid—she had remembered the lamp, even the flint and steel, but forgotten the belt she always wore in the day, and the little knife that hung from it.

A shadow moved apart from the rest. Rowan's eyes darted. Door—if she could get as far as that, and if it, he, whatever it was, did not know the baths as well as she—

The moon gave the shadow a face. Black mane of hair, black pits of eyes, sharp hawk-curve of nose.

"Kerrec!" Rowan's fear was gone all at once, in white rage. "What in the name of all the angels and saints are you doing here?"

"Who is that," he asked as if he had not heard her, "standing behind you?"

She whipped about. No one. Nothing. Only moonlight and darkness. She spun back, more furious than ever.

"She's beautiful," said Kerrec. "Strong, too. She looks like you. Your mother?"

Chill ran down Rowan's spine, even through her

temper. It was the way he said it: so calm; so strange in that light, with his face bleached pale and his eyes all the darker for it, fixed on a form that she could not see.

"There's nothing there," she said, loud and angry. "Nothing and no one."

"You know there is," he said. "You don't have the sight, I can see that. But you feel it. That's better than eyes, some ways. Less distracting."

"You're mad."

He smiled. "Moon-mad?"

He looked completely different when he smiled. All the sulkiness went away, and the tightness that made his whole face seem a backdrop for his beak of a nose.

"Did you follow me?" Rowan demanded, the sharper for that she had almost weakened and found him worth liking.

"I came where the moon was," he said.

Touched, definitely touched. "The moon is in the sky," said Rowan with elaborate patience.

"It's in the water," said Kerrec. "You feel the magic here. This is water that comes from the womb of the earth, heated in her fires. Moon touches it—that's air, and sky. All the elements in a single place."

"You *are* a witch," Rowan said. She thought about backing away, but failed to see the use in it. If he was going to bespell her, he would do it wherever she fled.

"Yes," he said, "I am a witch, and the son of a witch. She was a great lady of the Bretons, a princess of the old people. My father was a Frank."

"Of the House of Roland, I suppose," Rowan muttered.

Something of the mooncalf madness went out of his face, and the old bitter twist came back. "He was the great Count's kin. He had honor enough, until it was taken from him."

"That's how it always is in stories," Rowan said. "One's father is never a stableman or an honest tanner. He has to be a nobleman. Dishonored, of course. Or—"

"Sometimes the stories are true," said Kerrec. "Though what would you know of that? You've never had a moment's pain. Your father is lord of the world. Mine is dead. He died because of a coward and a fool. And that coward, that fool—he took my father's honor and claimed it for himself, and gave my father his own dishonor, because my father was dead and could say nothing."

"Then how do you know?" Rowan demanded.

He looked at her with those black eyes, the eyes he must have had from his mother. "How do you think I know?"

"You couldn't save him, then, you and your mother?"

He stepped back shaking, and dropped to his knees. His fists struck the tiles of the floor as he must have wanted to strike Rowan. "He was all the way across the empire in the Saxons' country. We could only watch. We saw him lead his men in glory. We saw the coward turn tail and run, and my father spur after him, and haul him back by the scruff of his craven neck, and throw him down. But he was clever, that snake of a man. He got a grip on my father's foot, and when he went down, my father went with him. The snake got up. My father never did. He had a Frankish dagger in his back. Because, the snake said,

45

my father was running away, and he fought the snake, who tried to call him back, and there was no help for it. And they believed the snake, because my father was dead, and couldn't speak for himself."

"People must have seen," Rowan said. "His men—"

"His men all died. The snake saw to that, too. There was no one left to tell the truth. Who was to doubt the liar? The one he told lies of was a marcher lordling mated to a witch of the old people, and the liar was noble Frank clear back to Merovech, with a wife as nobly Frank as he was, and an army of kin to stand behind him. For us there was only Roland, dead a dozen years, and a few weak cousins who were ashamed to be seen with us."

"And you," said Rowan.

"I was hardly weaned," Kerrec said. His anger was gone, or gone cold.

"Who was it?" Rowan asked. "Who did that terrible thing?"

"Does it matter?"

She planted her fists on her hips. "You've been waking the dead with your outrage, and now you say it doesn't matter?"

His lips stretched back from his teeth. It was not a smile. "That's exactly it, princess. My father's murderer is dead."

"Dead? But—"

"Yes, I came too late. By all accounts he died peacefully in his bed, with his soul duly shriven and his place in heaven assured." Kerrec did not even sound angry, only bitter, and tired.

46

"That's not fair," said Rowan.

"Should it be?"

"Yes," said Rowan. "Did you come to kill him?"

"No," said Kerrec. "Yes. It doesn't matter, does it? My enemy is dead. My father is dead. My mother is dead. My family's honor is dead. And here where there might be mending for all of that, what am I but an elephant's keeper?"

"That's not so little a thing," Rowan said. "You can talk to my father. He'll make it right."

"As easy as that?" Kerrec sat on his heels and sighed. "Let it be. Maybe it's best that I be no one here. I can prove myself as myself, and not as my father's son."

She did not say anything to that.

"You don't understand, do you?" he said. "But you do believe me."

She did understand: better maybe than he could imagine. And she did believe him. "Liars are smoother," she said, "and don't bother with me. They go to Bertha, who's the oldest, or Gisela, who's the favorite. And they don't . . . *feel* the way you do."

Either he understood, or he was too tired to wonder what she meant. He looked terrible. She wondered if he ever slept, or if he lay awake all night long, brooding on his troubles.

His eyes blurred in the lamp's light. They really were black, not brown, not simply all iris in the dimness. She had never seen eyes quite like that before. But then she had never seen a witch, either, or at least anyone who admitted to it.

She should be more afraid than she was. When he scuttled on hands and knees to the pool's edge, she followed, keeping a careful distance, but not too much of one. He bent over the water. The moon came right down into it. He reached as if to touch, but stopped short of it. He breathed on the water, and his breath, instead of ruffling it, stroked it hollow and smooth. The moon spilled into the bowl that he had made, filling it full.

Rowan was on her knees beside him. She did not remember kneeling. She certainly did not remember taking his hand. His dark thin fingers wound with her plumper, paler ones.

"Look," he said.

The moon was in the water. She could not see any more than that. She did not want to see any more than that.

"See," said the witch from Brittany. "A chamber, rich as a king's, and every hanging and carpet is purple when it's not gold. There's a bed, look, and people standing about it, and a woman in it. She's not old, not terribly, but she's very dead."

Rowan could not see, but as he spoke, she knew what he was seeing—knew as clearly as she knew her prayers. "That's the Empress," she said, slowly at first, because she had half decided to be horrified by the strangeness that had come over her. But once she had started, she found she could not stop. "That's Empress Irene in Byzantium. She's dead. They deposed her, and then they killed her, but they made it look as if she died all by herself. Is there someone standing near her—a man whose shoes are red?"

48

"He's standing over her," said Kerrec. "He's smiling."

"He's the one who had her killed. He's the Emperor now." Rowan's eyes went wide. "Then the danger is gone. The Empress of the East is dead. She can't marry my father. She can't cast a spell on him, or poison him, or—"

"The danger is greater than ever," Kerrec said, "if there's an Emperor in the East. An Empress might marry a man who calls himself Emperor of the West. An Emperor of the East, who wants to be Emperor of the world— he'll kill anyone he reckons a rival."

"Not my father," Rowan said.

"Not yet." Kerrec peered into the pool. "That's Michael Phokias. Look, he's talking to the man in the red shoes—but the man's shoes aren't red, yet. He's giving something to Michael Phokias."

"Gold," said Rowan, no longer even wondering that she knew, "in a purse. And orders. So the Byzantine isn't the Empress' man. He's the other's—the new Emperor's. He's to—to—" She gasped. "He's supposed to do something to my father."

"Kill him," said Kerrec.

"No," said Rowan, but the thing that made her know so much also made her helpless to deny the truth. "Not . . . all at once."

Kerrec was too intent on the pool to answer. "Gold. There's gold in the water. Jewels, crystal—the Talisman."

Rowan shuddered so hard that she almost fell into the pool. But Kerrec held her. She clung to him, both hands now, as hard as she could. "It's—it's not—" Oh, it hurt, to have those words tearing themselves out of her, and no way to stop them, no way not to say them, not to know what was in them. "If they get it, it will be deadly. I knew that; I felt it. What else it is—what it can do—it has more magic in it than anyone knows, even the Byzantine. But he knows enough. Once, only once, if the one who wears it has a pure heart, it can grant her—his—heart's desire. If he works on Gisela, if he gets her under his spell, he'll have what his master wants. He'll have my father."

Kerrec was silent. He was looking at her now and not at the water. A cloud ran across the moon. The bowl of his seeing melted and scattered.

Horror, held off too long, crashed down on her with trebled force. She had knelt in the middle of magic. She had been part of it. He could see, and she could not. But she could know what he saw. The two of them, joined hand in hand, were more than either one apart.

"I'm not a witch," she said. "I am—not—"

"You have the magic," said Kerrec.

She wrenched away from him. "You made me! You laid your spell on me."

"And you cast yours on me." *He* did not shudder at it. He was born for it. "The moon called you as it called me."

"No," said Rowan.

"We have to get the Talisman away from your sister," he said, "before she gives it to Michael Phokias."

"No," Rowan said again. She did not want to think

about what she had done, or what he had seen, or what she had known. There was magic in her. It ran in her blood. It pulsed under her skin. Her mother was never a witch, no, never. Her mother was a queen. Queens died and went to heaven. Witches went to hell.

She stumbled to her feet. The moon was gone. The water was dark. She plunged into it, as if water alone could make her clean. She scrubbed herself over and over.

Hands pulled at her. She fought them, but they were too strong. They dragged her out, raw skin and sopping shift and all, and wrapped her in something dry and vaguely warm, and shook her till the world came back again. The world was eyes. Eyes as black as the water without the moon, and a face gone white with fear.

The witch's son was afraid of her. No, not afraid of: afraid for. She laughed at that until she choked on it. "Tell me," she said, "that the moon's struck me mad."

"Not the moon," said Kerrec.

She pulled her wrappings tighter. She was cold to the bone, a cold that had nothing to do with the world's wind. "I can't do this. I can't be it."

"One isn't given a choice," Kerrec said.

Rowan shook her head. "I can't. You were born for it. I never was. Never—never—"

"Rowan," he said sharply. "Theoderada!"

He was trying to call her back to herself. But there was no self for him to call. Simple Rowan did not exist, except in wishes. Princess Theoderada was not a witch, not any kind of thing that stood handlinked with a witch's son and told him what he saw in a pool of moon and magic.

"Warn my father," she said. "Tell him to get back his Talisman. Tell him everything you know."

He looked very odd with his mouth agape. "But— you—"

She was moving already, walking at first, but each step was faster than the last. Away from him. Away from the water and the drowned moon.

"He won't listen to me!" Kerrec cried behind her. "It has to be you, Rowan. Rowan, damn it. Rowan!"

He would go to her father. Her father would listen. A man listened to a man, even if the one who talked was still mostly a boy. They did not need Rowan.

No one needed Rowan. Not even herself.

The night was dark, with the moon gone behind its cloud. More clouds came running out of the east. It would rain by morning. Then the heat would break, and the air be thin enough to breathe again.

Rowan paused in the garden. Sweetness of flowers warred with the stench of the midden. Kerrec had not followed her.

By the time he thought to run after her, she would be gone. All gone, all fled. Bravery was one thing, and fear for her father. Magic was too much to add to it.

The cloth she was wrapped in was her own gown. She put it on over her wet shift. Then, because she wanted to weep, she began to laugh. All that time, she had been as near to naked as made no difference, and Kerrec had not even noticed.

*R*OWAN BEGAN TO WONDER, midway through her flight, why she was so horrified. It did not do anything to stop her from running. Horses ran like that, once they had started, because it was easier to go on than to stop.

All her life people had been calling her mother a witch. All her life Rowan had been knowing things that nobody else knew, and hearing things that other people could not hear. She talked to her mother, after all, and her mother was dead.

But working magic, really working it, with someone who knew what it was, was too much for her to bear. It made the truth too clear. It proved what she had never wanted to prove.

So she ran. She ran right into the palace, to the chapel that had been her refuge before and was, for once, empty, and threw herself face down in front of the altar, struggling for breath. The floor was hard and cold. The vigil lamp burned low. The wooden Virgin was mute. Her mother was not there. She did not want her mother to be there, her mother the witch, who had bred magic in her daughter.

Rowan's breath came back soon enough, but her mind kept circling and circling, trying to fly out of itself.

She could not stay here, in Aachen, where this terrifying truth was. But where could she go?

She raised her head from her folded arms. The Virgin smiled her eternal smile.

Why, thought Rowan, of course. The one refuge that could protect her; the best refuge of all. Gisela wanted it, but lacked the fortitude to take it. The one for whom Gisela was named, their father's sister, had gone to it long ago. She was an abbess now, somewhere in the west of Francia.

Rowan would not have to go so far. Abbess Gisela had been in Aachen till a little while ago, visiting her brother and his children; then she had gone to Cologne, to a cloister there, to rest her head from the clamor of palaces, and to pray in peace where someone else was abbess. Cologne was close to Aachen, not much more than a day's ride.

Rowan sat up. Yes, she thought. She would go to Cologne. Aunt Gisela was wise, if not exactly kind, and she had known Rowan's mother well. She would know what to do.

Rowan went alone. She could hardly ask a servant to go with her, and her sisters would ask too many questions. She crept into the room she shared with Bertrada. The maid was there, sound asleep. Rowan gathered what she needed, moving as silently as she could, jumping every time Bertrada stirred. But the woman never woke. Softly, clutching the bundle of her belongings, Rowan slipped out of the room.

If Galla had been in the stable it would have been hard: it was almost time for the horses to wake and start demanding breakfast. But the pony was in the pasture just outside the walls, where there was a postern gate, and she was puzzled but not dismayed to find Rowan there at this unwonted hour. She took the bit willingly enough, blew out as she always did for the saddle, but Rowan was used to that. Rowan walked her forward, tightened the girth its usual three fingers' worth, and swung into the saddle, tugging at the fastenings of her bundle. They held; they would do. Galla was eager to go. She pranced, even, and snorted a little, to show that she was fresh.

Dawn was breaking as they took the road. Dark lingered under the trees that lined it, but it was the Emperor's road, broad and smooth, and the sides of it were kept clear of trees. No one met Rowan, and no one threatened her. She might have been alone in all the world, but for the pony under her and the birds that sang, greeting the rising sun.

Galla was half Arab, and she was both fast and strong, but no horse could go on all day at a gallop, if its rider cared for it at all. Out of sight of Aachen, where the road bent a little south of east and the trees closed in in places to overhang the track, Rowan slowed the pony to a trot, and then to a walk. Galla was still restive, tossing her head and sidling, shying at something in the trees. Rowan peered at first, wary enough herself to bolt, but she saw nothing, nor was there anything to hear. It was horse-silliness, that was all.

Rowan kicked her forward, a little harder than was strictly necessary. Galla started but did not buck. Rowan patted her neck, contrite.

Maybe, Rowan thought, she should go back. Her father had given away the Talisman that should have protected him, and he did not even know it.

"But what can I do?" she said to the air and the trees and Galla's finely turned ears. "I'm not a man, to fight with a sword, or a sorcerer, to fight with magic. I can pray, that's all. And prayer is best done on holy ground."

"You always have excuses, don't you?"

Galla stopped short, nearly throwing Rowan over her head, staring hard at a shadow among the treetrunks. It separated itself from a horde of its fellows and became a figure Rowan knew too well.

"How did you get here?" she snapped at him. "On a devil's back?"

"You could say that," said Kerrec mildly. A grey and wrinkled snake slithered out from behind him, with a wall of grey behind that, and a pale gleam of tusks.

Rowan's jaw had dropped. She shut her mouth with a snap, more angry than ever. "You stole my father's Elephant!"

"He was going to steal himself," Kerrec said. "I went with him to see where he was going. He's invisible in the dark, did you know? And as quiet as a cat."

"Witchcraft," said Rowan.

Galla snorted as the Elephant moved out into the road, towering over them all. Rowan could feel her trying to decide if she should bolt. A firm rein and a steady leg calmed her down, at least enough to go on with.

Kerrec took no notice of the negotiations. "Excuses or no excuses, you're turning tail and running away."

Rowan scraped together what dignity she could. Screaming at people never helped, not when they were looking at her with one eyebrow up and daring her to do something worth sneering at. "Is it any business of yours what I do or where I go?"

"Abbess Gisela left Cologne this morning," Kerrec said. "She's going back to her abbey at Chelles. You'd have to hurry to catch her—she took the road south of here."

"I could have you," Rowan said very deliberately, "cried as a witch and burned in the public square."

"Go ahead and do it," Kerrec said. His voice was perfectly calm. "I won't even denounce you. Think of living with that for the rest of your life."

Galla had gone still. "Move aside," Rowan said. Her voice was thin and tight. "Let me go."

Kerrec tilted a hand as if to indicate that he was not in her way. The Elephant was another matter. He had turned himself to bar the road, casually, as if he had nothing more on his mind than a trunkful of fresh green branches.

He was as high and solid as a wall, with an eye that rolled back at her and somehow managed to shame her utterly. "I can't stay," she said. It was more of a whine than she wanted it to be. "I can't help. Except to pray."

The Elephant's eye closed as if in scorn. He broke off a great hanging branch with a crack that made Rowan jump near out of her skin, but Galla never moved. With gentleness that was terrible next to that proof of his strength, he plucked the leaves from the branch and chewed them slowly, meditatively, and with every evidence of enjoyment.

Rowan could try to break through the trees and circle round him, but he could uproot them and come straight at her. She could abandon Galla and run right under him, and then he would catch her with a swoop of his trunk. He was leaving her no way to go but back to Aachen: back to fear, and to duty that she did not want.

If she had been on the ground, she would have stamped her foot. "Who do you think you are? Let me go!"

"Maybe he thinks that he protects your father," Kerrec said.

"But what can I do?" she cried.

"I don't know, I'm sure," said Kerrec dryly, "but Abul Abbas seems to think you're good for something."

"What? To peer into pools and tell you what you see?"

"That's what frightens you, isn't it?" he said. "You're more than you thought you were. You can't think of anything to do but run away from it."

Rowan flung herself down from Galla's back. She

had just enough wits left to keep a grip on the reins, or she would have launched herself into him, kicking and spitting. "Maybe I'm the danger to my father. Have you thought of that? What if they get hold of me, and use me against him?"

"Nonsense," said Kerrec. "They've got Gisela. What do they need you for? You're a coward, that's all. Your father needs you, and what can you think of to do but run away and leave him to it?"

"*I'm* a coward?" Rowan sucked in her breath. The rest of it came out by itself, without any help from her. "Oh, you would know, wouldn't you, Kerrec of the Bretons?"

His face was quite pale and quite still, and quite terrifying. He would kill her, she thought. She was not afraid. It was fascinating to see that there was so much to him after all. So much fire. So much rage, so pure that it was white. It transformed him. Maybe this was what the Basques had seen of his cousin Roland at Roncesvalles, before they died at his hands.

Then he moved, and he was Kerrec again, a half-fledged boy-man in a ragged shirt, with an elephant standing behind him. "One would think," he said coldly, "that I would know. Wouldn't I?"

Shame burned her cheeks. It started with Kerrec, but it ran through everything else, till she would have gladly died.

"There now," he said in his soft Breton lilt. "You were afraid; you had every right to be. It's terrifying, after all, to be so strong, and never to have known. And everybody teaching you that it's an ill thing, and mocking your mother's memory. Of course you ran away."

That brought her back to life again, and temper too. "I don't need your sympathy!"

"Then you'll get it unneeded," said Kerrec. "If you go back now, people won't ask too many questions. We've been out exercising the Elephant, haven't we, and your pony needed a run. Is that breakfast in your saddlebag? We could eat it, you know, and be convincing."

"I hate you," said Rowan, but without force.

"That's better than indifference," said Kerrec.

She would never best him in a war of words. She did not know why she had to keep trying. Stubbornness, she supposed. She had enough of that for a troop of runaway princesses.

Seven

R OWAN GOT a tongue-lashing for running out unan-
nounced, but it was no worse than usual, and everybody
settled down soon enough. They had more than her delin-
quencies to occupy them, with the palace still so full of
people. And the Elephant's house was ready at last, which
she had been too preoccupied to notice.

Abul Abbas would not escape so easily now. Instead
of the stable with its open courtyards and its gates that
were always seeing people come and go, he was given a
place in the big half-wooded park of the Emperor's menagerie, with a tall wooden building for him to sleep in.
The gates here were barred, and the most dangerous or
the most flighty creatures lived in cages: the lion, the
leopard, the birds that sang and the birds that were merely
brilliant to look at. Abul Abbas had his house with its
great door that could be barred to keep him in or left open
to let the air blow through, with his own bit of yard to
walk in. Sometimes he came out into the wider space of
the park, with Kerrec riding on his neck. Children were
always asking and grown noblemen demanding to ride in

the litter that was made for the Elephant's back, and once in a while Kerrec allowed it. He was growing princely, was Kerrec, for being the Elephant's keeper.

Rowan stayed away from both of them. She cherished a conviction that if she did not speak to them, did not look at them, did not think about them, the magic in her would go away.

And so it seemed to. She did not even talk to her mother's memory. She was as close to just-Rowan as the Princess Theoderada could be, going to lessons in the school, attending her father at dinner, stitching at her altar cloth.

But Rowan did not ride her pony, who grew fat and bored in the pasture, and bit one of the grooms who brought her in to work a knot of burrs out of her mane. Rowan was not going to do anything that would jar loose the delicate balance of her ordinariness.

The longer she went on being so ordinary, the more she felt as if she were a peasant girl with a jar of milk on her head, and if she slipped or stumbled the jar would come crashing down. Her neck was stiff with the effort, and her stomach was knotted tight.

She went to bed at sundown with the rest of the women, and did not go out to bathe in the moonlight, no matter how tempting it was. She was just Rowan. She was safe, and her father was safe, and the Talisman was in no danger, living on its chain around Gisela's neck.

"Hist! Rowan!"

Rowan started, and yelped. Her needle had jabbed her finger so hard it drew blood.

"Rowan," the whisper came again.

Curiosity was her besetting flaw. She had to turn. She had to see the head framed in the window of the women's gallery, tousled and spiky and permanently annoyed.

She resisted the urge to gape. Either Kerrec had sprouted wings, or he was perched on the fragile support of the grapevine that ran along the top of the portico. Either way, he was standing a good three man-heights above the ground, where he had no business to be. She turned her back on him.

"Rowan," he said in a more normal voice, if still soft—he must have seen that she was alone with her embroidery and her basket of silks and the dapple of sun on the polished wooden floor. "Rowan, do you know where your sister is?"

A really wise woman would have ignored him completely. Rowan had never been wise. "Which one?" she asked the wall opposite. "I have an army of them."

"You know which one," said Kerrec with his best imitation of patience.

"I suppose she's out with the others," Rowan said, "picking berries in the wood."

He did not ask why Rowan had not gone with them. She wished he would, so that she could snap his head off properly.

There was a scuffle and a soft thump. She knew without looking that he was in the room, breathless, cursing softly at a barked shin or a skinned elbow.

"You'll get your hide tanned if anyone finds you here," Rowan said with some pleasure. "Or worse."

"Sometimes," said Kerrec, "I wonder if all budding

girls are like mares out of season, squealing and kicking at any male that happens by. Do you do it because you want to, or because you think you have to?"

A flush crawled up Rowan's cheeks. She decided to call it anger. "Why should I answer you?"

Maybe he shrugged. She refused to look. "You might care where the Princess Gisela is. She's not in the wood. They all think she's gone to pray, but she's not in the chapel, either, or anywhere else that's holy."

Rowan found that her hands were shaking. She set down her embroidery before she drew blood again, sheathed the needle in a bit of cloth, and knotted her fingers in her lap. "Why did you come to me? What can I do that my father's guards can't?"

"You want me to be the one to say it, don't you?"

Her eyes came up of their own accord. Kerrec looked much as he always did, like a half-fledged hawk. He was quite homely, she thought, beaky and untidy. He smelled, faintly but distinctly, of elephant.

But none of that mattered with those black eyes on her, challenging her, naming her the coward that she was. The Elephant had not let her run away to Cologne, but she had run away into herself.

"You don't understand," she said. "You were brought up to it. I was taught to shrink from it."

"From what? Courage?"

"Now you're the one who's playing the fool."

"So say it. Say what you're afraid of."

She drew a deep breath. She was not going to. No. Not the word.

It came out by itself. "Magic," she said in a soft

64

voice that was worse somehow than a scream. "Magic, magic, magic!"

He nodded, unruffled. "Magic," he agreed. "You can't hide it, you know, not from anyone who can see. You can only hide it from yourself."

"What," she asked with bitter humor, "do I blaze like a beacon in the dark?"

"More like a candle in a gale," said Kerrec. He reached and, with daring so mighty it was irresistible, pulled her to her feet. "Come on. And pray we're not too late."

Rowan tried to dig in her heels. He was too strong, and he was moving too fast. She stumbled after him, willy-nilly, out of the gallery, down the back stair, into the dim and musty servants' corridors. If they passed any servants, she was too stark with mingled rage and fear to notice.

Her veil got lost somewhere. The crown of her braids uncoiled and tumbled down her back. Kerrec was running, his grip on her hand tight enough to bruise.

And because he was touching her, because there was no getting away from the magic no matter what she did, she knew something of why he ran. The Elephant—the Talisman—

She tried to wrench loose. She managed to slow them both down a little, and to spin him half around, but he only spun back and kept on going, right out of the palace into dim reaches of courtyards, round the royal reek of the kitchen midden and through a gate and into the orchard.

And then he stopped, as sudden as if he had struck

a wall. Rowan fell to her knees. They were both gasping for breath, and she was too furious to see anything but his sweating face. "What in the name of—" she began, and not softly, either.

His hand clapped over her mouth. She tried to twist her head around and bite, but he was too clever, or too experienced. "Stop it!" he hissed in her ear. "They'll hear us."

She had been steaming hot, but all at once she was cold. She turned very carefully. Kerrec did not try to stop her, though he kept his hand over her mouth.

There they were under the tree that Rowan loved. They looked like innocent lovers. Gisela's head was in the Byzantine's lap. He was stroking her loosened hair, stroking and stroking it, and under his hand that lay on her breast was a gleam of gold. As he stroked her hair he sang, his voice as soft as sleep, buzzing like bees in a lazy noon, setting all thoughts free to drift, drift . . .

"Rowan!"

Kerrec's voice was like shattering glass. Rowan found herself clinging to him, half ready to fall over. Kerrec of course was wide awake. While she was still gaping and gasping, he pulled her behind a tree. "What—" she tried to say. "How—"

"That's a sleep-sorcery," Kerrec said, as if Rowan could not have guessed. "There, he has her."

Rowan started out from behind the tree. Kerrec pulled her back. "Not like that, idiot. That's magic he's using— strong magic. You can't fight it by blundering right into it."

"Then what am I supposed to do?" Rowan demanded, trying to whisper and shout at the same time. "I can't just watch him take the Talisman!"

"You might have to," said Kerrec.

"Then what—" Rowan said again, but stopped. What was the use? She peered carefully round the treetrunk. Gisela was sound asleep. Michael Phokias paused as if to admire his handiwork, or maybe he was human enough to be struck by her beauty as she lay there, all white and silvery gold. Carefully then, with fingers gloved in silk, he lifted the Talisman from her breast.

Rowan held her breath. He did not reel or cry out, nor did he fall over dead. He took the Talisman and held it up. "And this," he asked in a voice that still held memories of his spellcasting, "is your free gift to me?"

"Yes," said Gisela drowsily. "It is my free gift to you."

"To keep and to guard, and to wield as it best pleases me?"

"To keep and to guard," she repeated in her sleep, "and to wield as it best pleases you."

"Then sleep," he said, and maybe that was triumph in his voice, rigidly clamped down or he would break the spell. "Sleep and be at peace. There is nothing in the world to fear, nothing to remember but that you had a relic, and you grew weary of it, and put it away with all the rest."

"Nothing," murmured Gisela. "Weary. Put . . . away. . ."

Cautiously Michael Phokias slid from beneath Gisela. She sighed and stirred, and Rowan dared to hope that she would wake, but she only curled like a kitten and tucked her hand beneath her head and fell deeper asleep. Michael Phokias smiled down at her. "Dream well, my beautiful witling," he said.

He plucked a bit of silk from his sleeve and wrapped the Talisman in it, but not before he paused to admire the gleam of sun in its colored stones. "Beautiful," he said to it in Greek. "O beautiful." He was purring with satisfaction. He returned the silk to his sleeve, and the Talisman with it, smoothed his robes and straightened his hat and preened his curly beard. Then he turned toward the tree that—however inadequately—hid both Rowan and Kerrec.

She made herself as narrow as she could, and tried not to breathe. Kerrec, who was no wider than the tree, stepped out from behind it before she could stop him, and sauntered toward the sorcerer.

Michael Phokias paused. If he was angry or dismayed, he did not show it. His nose went up a fraction, as if he detected the scent of elephant on the Elephant's boy, and did not find it pleasing.

Kerrec halted as if startled—Rowan caught the edge of it as she craned around the tree. He ducked clumsily, as a peasant might bow, except that no peasant would be that awkward, and squeaked like the boy he no longer really was. "My lord! My lord, what—" He seemed to catch sight of Gisela. His voice went up another half-octave. "My lady! Is she ill? Is she dead? I'll fetch the servants—the guards—the physicians—"

The Byzantine's voice cut through his babbling. "She

is sleeping. I found her so; I trust that you will leave her to it."

Kerrec yattered on. "Somebody's been trying to—trying to—to—*force* her? Guards!"

That might have been a shout, in something near his natural tone, if the Byzantine had not tripped him so neatly that it might have looked like an accident: the gawky boy hopping and fretting, catching his foot on the man's and falling flat on his face. Except that Kerrec was not gawky, no matter how many extra knees and elbows he seemed to have, and he only stumbled and caught himself on the man's robes.

Rowan was not breathing. Kerrec was putting on a show fit to make a cutpurse proud, but the Byzantine was too slippery for him. He slithered out from under Kerrec's hands, set him on his feet, wrinkled his fine nose again at the stink of commoner—little as he knew the truth of that—and said, "Boy, have you been at your betters' wine? For shame! and you so young. Here, stand up straight, draw a breath, yes. Yes!"

And as he said it he patted Kerrec all over, as if to be sure that he had not hurt himself, straightening the ragged tunic and refastening the worn belt and smoothing the hair that went wherever it willed. Kerrec must have been hard put to maintain his expression of bucolic stupidity. There was a white tinge about his nostrils.

He was going to lose his temper. Rowan felt it like a bonfire on her face. Too fast even to think, she flounced out from behind the tree, calling, "Kerrec! Kerrec, you mooncalf, what are you bothering his excellency for?"

Not all the heat in that place was Kerrec's anger

rising. There was something added to it, something with a tang like hot iron. Magic. It lay in Michael Phokias' hands, wound about Kerrec as he stood immobile, and maybe he could not move if he had wanted to.

Michael Phokias was looking a little ruffled. Rowan gave him no time to speak. "My lord, you have to pardon him, he fancies himself clever. Not that he isn't, mind you," she said with the best simper she could manage — it turned Kerrec faintly green — "but he does get a little above himself. He likes to think that he can guard a lady's virtue. Charming, isn't it? He's only an elephant's boy." She patted him as if he had been her dog, trying not to flinch when her hand touched magic. It felt like ice wound with fire. It itched inside her skin. "But charming, as I said. And very much more interesting than he looks."

"I hope for your sake, my lady," said Michael Phokias, "that he is."

Rowan smiled, she hoped sweetly. "Oh, I like them when they're young and awkward. They're so new to it, you see. So energetic. And so grateful to be noticed." She widened her eyes, all innocence. "I don't suppose you know about that. Gisela has always preferred them a little more seasoned. Do you mind giving her back her relic? Father will be so annoyed if he finds out she's given it away."

Kerrec's breath stopped short. Michael Phokias seemed briefly, much too briefly, at a loss. But his tongue was supple, and he had no shame that she could see. "Oh, you saw that, did you, my lady? She entrusted it to

70

me for safekeeping. It's very valuable, you know. Much more valuable than she seems to understand."

"I'm sure she doesn't understand," Rowan said. Her heart was pounding hard, but she had gone too far to stop. "Really, I think it would be best if it went back to our father's treasury. What if the Caliph discovers that a man of Byzantium has taken it? He might put the wrong interpretation on it. And Byzantium is so much closer to him than we, so much easier to attack."

"I doubt that that will happen, my lady," said Michael Phokias. "This relic is safe with me. I give you my word on it."

The word of a sorcerer. Rowan was not quite mad enough to say that, even now. "It will be safer in the treasury," she said, "your excellency. As I'm sure my father will agree."

There. Let him read that for a threat. He smiled slightly, one might almost have thought kindly. "Perhaps he may. Meanwhile, I shall guard the relic with all the care that it deserves, against the day that he will ask it of me."

"I think it best that I be the one to guard it," Rowan said, holding out her hand. "If you please, my lord?"

"My lady," he said, still sweetly, still smoothly, "I think not. It was never meant for a woman's gentle hand. What if it should wake, and burn you to the bone? Such tender white skin, to be so marred."

"No Christian relic ever burned a Christian hand," said Rowan.

"Did I say that this was Christian?" asked Michael

Phokias. "No, no, princess. The Caliph may be your father's friend, but this is no friendly thing. Believe me when I tell you that it were best under guard, and far from your father's hand."

"How do you know?" Rowan asked him. "Are you a sorcerer?"

Even that did not take him aback for more than a instant. "Why, princess, I know a little of the hidden arts. So does any educated man. This is a work of those arts, and not of their gentler face, either. Come, continue your tryst with your clever ragged boy, and trust that I shall do as I best may, to guard this relic from the East."

He did not lay any spell on her that she knew of, but she could not stop him as he walked past her, bowing to her ladyship, taking the Talisman away.

When she could move again, he was gone, and Kerrec was spitting with rage. "Why in the name of every saint and angel did you tell him everything we knew?"

"Because," said Rowan, too tired and drained to be angry, "I thought it would do some good. You didn't get it away from him, did you?"

"No," Kerrec snapped, clenching and unclenching his fists. One of them looked red and blistered.

Rowan would hardly spare him any sympathy, but it did bear mentioning. "You touched it?"

"I touched something," he said. "He's got it wrapped in sorceries already. If he hadn't, I could have plucked it, neat as a bezant from a drunken prince's purse."

Rowan got hold of his hand, though he tried to evade

her. It was blistered indeed, as if he had caught it in a fire. "You'll want a salve for this. And not a squeak out of you. It's a wonder he didn't see it, and understand it all."

"It's a wonder he didn't catch on when you told him everything. What ever possessed you to yatter on like that?"

"Prudence," said Rowan. "Hiding in plain sight. He has us marked now. You're my peasant paramour. I'm the princess who prics where she shouldn't."

"So you are," growled Kerrec.

"I had to try," she said, stubborn. "He might have given in."

"And the trees might have stood up and walked." Kerrec dropped down in a tangle of legs and arms. "He knows we know, now. And he has the Talisman."

"But can he do anything with it?"

"Would he have taken it if he couldn't?" Kerrec worked fingers into his hair, rumpling it worse than ever. "We should both have kept quiet and watched, and then gone to find someone to help."

"Who?" Rowan demanded. "A priest? A philosopher? Old Hilde the herbwoman?"

"Hilde might know how to put a sorcerer to sleep and steal what he's stolen from your sister."

"Hilde has no magic in her at all." Rowan had not known it till she said it. The magic was loose again. She did not know how to stop it. "There isn't anyone, Kerrec. There's only us."

"There's your father," said Kerrec.

"No," said Rowan. "When I tried to warn him, he

73

wouldn't listen. What makes you think he'll pay any more attention now?"

"It might make a difference to him that your sister has lost the Talisman."

Rowan shook her head. "Even if he did decide to listen — what if it's a trap? What if we're supposed to run to him, and catch him in the Byzantine's spell?"

That stopped Kerrec, at least for a moment. Rowan pressed on through his silence. "Is there someone in Brittany who can help?"

Kerrec looked as if he might have said more about the Emperor, but he answered Rowan's question instead. "Not soon enough," he said. "We can't fly. We're not that kind of witches."

"You're not much of any kind of witch, are you?" she said bitterly. "You can see things in pools, that's all, and play cutpurse's tricks."

"Can you do any more?"

She glared at him. For some reason her eyes were full of tears. She swept her hand up, then down. Chains of magic shredded and tore. "I don't know what I can do. I don't want to know. But I have to, don't I? I can't get away from it."

"This time I wouldn't stop you if you ran away. The Elephant might, but if you start now, you can outrun him."

It was tempting. Oh, it was a beautiful thought, to saddle Galla and ride away from everything.

Too late now for that. She had seen the Talisman in Michael Phokias' hand. She had to get it away from him. She did not even care why. She had to, that was all.

She looked at Kerrec. He stared back, mute for once. "You can't touch the Talisman. He was right in that much—it will burn. But maybe I can. It was made for my father, wasn't it? And I'm his seed. If anyone gets it back, it has to be me."

"And I called you a coward," said Kerrec, as if to himself.

"Oh, I am," Rowan said. "I'm dead stark terrified of what that man will do if he keeps the Talisman long enough to use it."

"But we couldn't get it away from him when he was caught off guard. How can we get it now that he knows we know?"

"I don't know," said Rowan, "but I'll think of something."

Kerrec did not have a very high opinion of her resourcefulness, from the look on his face. Neither did she. But it was the best that anyone could do. It would have to be enough.

Eight

ROWAN TRIED TO SLEEP.

Bertrada, as usual, was snoring. Rowan never minded it much, but tonight, the longer it went on, the more she wanted to scream.

She had kept herself admirably in hand, she thought, through all of that interminable day. She had even been able to eat dinner not a spearlength from the sorcerer, as outwardly calm as he was, or so she hoped, although she paid for it now: her stomach felt as hard and cold as a stone.

Rowan could not sleep, but she could not get up, either. Where could she go? The chapel was full of her mother's memory. The baths were terrible with the remembrance of magic. The gallery still echoed with Kerrec's presence.

Her back ached with trying not to move. Carefully she turned onto her side. Her shoulder started to ache. She lay on her stomach. She never had been comfortable sleeping that way. She tried lying on her back again.

None of it did any good. She got up, pulled on her

shift and then her gown. Bertrada's snoring changed tempo. She muttered, flailed, and sprawled across the whole of the bed.

Even with no moon to vex Rowan's magic, the dark had a power of its own. But fear or no fear, memories or no memories, she had to get out.

She was not at all surprised to find Kerrec sitting on the rim of the fountain in the women's court. There was just enough starlight to see the fall of the fountain, and the shape in shadow that was Kerrec.

"He's using the Talisman," Kerrec said without greeting, as if no time had passed since the morning.

"You *see* him?" Rowan asked. Her voice was shaky.

"I don't need to. I feel it. Don't you? Or did you just come out here to bay at the moon?"

"There isn't any moon," said Rowan, sharp with mingled anger and fear.

"No moon," he agreed, impervious to her temper, "but magic enough."

Rowan did not need him to tell her that. Her skin was all aprickle with it. "So? And what do you intend to do about it?"

"Nothing," he said. "There's nothing anyone can do."

"Nothing?" she echoed, incredulous. "Nothing at all? *You* can say—" She broke off, and peered hard at him. He was a shape of dark on dark, not even light enough to see the pale smudge of his face. No, she had not imagined it, or misheard. He had sounded quenched, all his sharp edges gone blunt with despair.

"What did you try to do?" she demanded. "Did you

try to get the Talisman again? He laid a spell on you, didn't he?"

Kerrec did not say anything. Maybe he shrugged.

Rowan seized his shoulders. They were thin, brittle-boned like a bird's. "He did. Didn't he?"

"I didn't . . . do anything." Kerrec had trouble getting it out, maybe because Rowan was shaking him so hard. "I just . . . watched by his door. And let him see me do it."

Rowan's breath hissed between her teeth. "That was unbelievably stupid."

"Not any more stupid than you telling him everything." There was a little more life in Kerrec's voice. Yes, thought Rowan: get his pride up. Make him angry enough to shake off whatever it was that sucked the life out of him. "We can't storm his room and demand the thing back, can we?"

"My father can," said Rowan.

He made a disgusted noise. "You're the one who said we shouldn't try—he'd just tell you to stop fretting, and then forget all about it."

"So I made a mistake," Rowan snapped. "So I've had time to think. Get up and come with me."

"Where? To beard the sorcerer in his lair?"

"No," said Rowan with heroic patience. "To watch over my father. Unless you're pickpocket enough to steal the Talisman from the sorcerer in the middle of his working?"

"I'm not a thief!"

There. That was Kerrec, prickles and all, and never

mind that he had tried to do just that, this past morning. Rowan was too scared to be relieved. It was crazy to imagine that either of them could do anything, crazier to try to do it at the target instead of at the weapon. But they had tried to face the Byzantine when he was off guard, lazy with complacency, and not yet fully in possession of the Talisman. Now he had had time to build his fortifications. An archbishop with book and candle might have knocked them down, but no archbishop Rowan knew of would listen to a pair of children. Especially a pair of children who confessed to witchcraft.

She could only hope that if they stayed near her father, they could protect him from harm. She could only pray that it was not too late. She should have been on guard since she left the garden, not dithering and fretting and being no use at all.

She was still dithering. She scrambled herself together and went where she should have gone long hours ago.

The Emperor had rooms in the palace's heart, with strong guards on them, full-armed and armored. The men in the armor were friends of Rowan's; she had known them since she was a baby. They were not used to seeing her there at such an hour, but they were not suspicious either, even of Kerrec stalking stiffly in her shadow. Kerrec was not wearing his ragged elephant's-boy clothes tonight; this tunic was plain but well and richly made, and he had combed his hair, and he had a short sword in a sheath at his side. Rowan wondered if he had been trying to pass for someone who belonged in the sorcerer's company. Or maybe he had been going courting when he smelled the reek of magic.

She did not think she liked that last thought.

Whatever had made him change his clothes, he looked like the lord's son he was, for once. A princess could well seem to ask for his company as she wandered the corridors at night.

Kerrec kept quiet as Rowan talked her way past the guards. "His majesty's asleep, then?" she asked as innocently as she could.

"Sound asleep," said Bodo, who had been the love of her life when she was five years old and he was as tall as the moon. Now he was just a little taller than she was, and growing bald; but he was still her friend, insofar as a guard could be friend to a princess. "He came to bed late, just fell right in, and no company there, either."

Rowan drew a small breath of relief. That was often a concern, with the Emperor; he did not like to sleep alone. "Oh, he's lucky," she said. "I couldn't sleep at all, and there's nothing to read in the women's hall. I thought I'd find something in his library that might put me to sleep."

She widened her eyes a little as she spoke, not too much, just enough to look innocent. In fact she had raided her father's library before, if never quite so late; she was wagering that Bodo would remember, and not ask questions.

"Well," he said, "I suppose I can let you in. If you promise you won't wake him up?"

"If he's asleep," said Rowan with perfect sincerity, "I'll be as quiet as a cat."

"Well then," said Bodo, "in you go."

In, then, she went, with Kerrec following like her shadow. Bodo had not asked about him. She wondered if the guard had even seen the Elephant's boy, or recognized him.

Not that it mattered, once they were in, and a good strong guard on the doors behind them. Rowan did not go into the Emperor's bedchamber, though she paused by the door. The squire who lay across it woke, grinned drowsily till he saw Kerrec, then wiped all expression from his face. Rowan ignored him.

The nightlamp was lit in the Emperor's room, flickering in the draft from the door. She could not see into the big curtained bed, but she could hear the noble rasp of her father's snore. She paused for a long while, listening to that blessed rhythm, before she retreated from the doorway. She kept her promise to Bodo: she moved as softly as she knew how.

Next to her father's sleeping-room was the one where he kept his books, with a table to sit at, and a chair with a tattered silken cushion, and a locked chest for the books. Rowan unlatched the door with the minutest of clicks, and slid into the room. She had not been lying to Bodo about where she intended to go, though she had not told him all the reasons why she went. Truth, she thought, was a complicated thing.

There was a lamp lit on the table, as there always was: the Emperor never knew when he might want to get up in the night and practice his reading or his writing. He had been writing earlier, perhaps just before he went to bed. There was a scrap of parchment on the table, with what looked like a tribute-list on one side, and a line of scribbles on the other. He had tried so hard that the tip of the quill splayed, making the letters at the end of the line much darker and larger than the ones at the beginning, and spattering ink on the bottom of the parchment.

Rowan's eyes pricked with tears. Fear of losing her father was a thing of such magnitude that she could only face it by sniffling over small things. The white starkness of Kerrec's face. The sound of her father's snores. This bit of parchment with its marks of earnest intensity, its remembrance of a man who learned to read late in life, came later still to writing and yet persevered. He had an empire full of scribes to do his reading and writing for him, and children whom he had raised to be as learned as he had never been, but still he copied these scraps of Ovid and Cicero, determined to write them with his own hand.

The Byzantines would despise this if they knew of it. Rowan warmed with anger at the thought. Her father was worth twenty of any Greek yet born.

She sat in the chair and touched finger to the scrap of parchment. Maybe it was only fancy, but she thought that she could feel her father in it, like a thread that ran from her hand to the parchment to the man asleep in his bed on the other side of the wall. The thread was as thin as a spider's strand, and as nearly invisible, and yet it had color in it, maybe grey, maybe green, maybe a little of both. It made her think of something, but she was not quite sure what.

She felt rather than saw Kerrec come up behind her and lean on the chair's high back. He spoke in a whisper. "Do you know what you're doing?"

If she answered him, she would lose the thread. It was important that she not do that. He sensed it, maybe. He did not press her.

Somewhere far away from the center, part of her was shaking and sobbing and trying desperately to run away. But it was not the part that moved her body, or that held the thread in her hand. It was a very real thread, a length of silk: the odd-colored silk that she had been given in the market, the day she first sat on the Elephant. She had put that thread in her workbox and forgotten about it, since it was so odd a color, even if it matched her eyes. And yet here it was, in her hand. She knew the heft of it, the softness that was silk, the strength that hid in it and made it wonderful.

She felt Kerrec's hand on her shoulder, his presence like a wall at her back. He should be doing this, wailed the coward in her. He knew how to use magic. *He* should guard the thread, and let her go.

But she had seen the thread first, and she had touched it, and somehow made it real. She knew what she had to do. It was very simple. She had to hold the thread, and keep it from breaking.

Spots danced in front of her eyes. She shook her head to make them go away, but they kept on. Slowly

they came together. They were gold, green, red, white—
the Talisman with its jewels, and in its heart the holy
relic.

Only the gold was dim, tarnished. The jewels were
dull. The relic looked like a blot on the crystal, a sliver
of darkness that grew as she watched.

"That's the spell." Kerrec's voice, sounding strange
and far away. Had she sounded like that when she told
him what he saw in the water of the baths? "He's planted
it in the crystal, and commanded it to grow."

"But how?" part of Rowan asked, part that had voice
to speak. "There's a piece of God's own Tree in the stone.
How could he turn it so dark?"

"Anything holy can be twisted," said Kerrec. "And
this had magic in it to begin with."

"No," said Rowan. She was not talking to Kerrec.
She could see past the Talisman now, as if through a
window. The sorcerer had set the golden thing in a circle
drawn on the floor of a dim and shadowy room. He stood
outside the circle, robed in darkness, and chanted words
that, by the mercy of heaven, she could not hear. But she
could feel them, buzzing like wasps in her skull.

Something warned her to back away, to close her
ears, to turn her focus entirely on the Talisman. Its gold
was gone. It looked like lead, dull and drab, and the
stones were like river pebbles. The crystal was black.

Rowan swallowed a cry of protest. She had not loved
that splendid frightening thing, but it had been beautiful
and magical and holy. Now it was all wrong, all twisted.
Where the wood of the Cross had been was a demon's

eye. It leered at her, seeing every speck and folly of her, and knowing her for what she was.

"Mary Mother of God!"

Rowan had not thought at all before the words were out, but they rang like bells in the night. The demon's eye closed against them. Its spell broke, setting her free.

She saw the Talisman still, blackened and fouled. A thread spun out of it, a black thread, like a shadow of Rowan's grey-green living silk. It unrolled through the dim air, aiming straight and level and swift as an arrow's flight, direct to her father's chamber.

Prayer did not slow it, not even the whole Paternoster. Just at "deliver us from evil," the black thread touched the thread of the Emperor's life. And stopped.

Rowan did not dare to hope. Not yet. Where the two threads met was a point half of shadow and half of light. The one in her hand was like a hot wire, so hot it burned, but not for any pain would she let go. Her body was between the black thread and her father. If it came on, it must come on through her.

Through her and Kerrec. He felt more solid than ever, standing behind her, saying nothing, doing nothing but hold fast.

The blackness moved, creeping toward her. Her teeth met in her lower lip. The pain, like the pain in her hand, helped her to focus. She kept praying. It did not seem to do any good, but neither did it hurt. If she prayed enough, maybe she would be so full of holiness that when the blackness touched her it would shrivel and die.

The living thread darkened inch by inch. It was

coming faster now. Her hand was on fire. Her head was throbbing. She could not remember the words of the prayer she was saying. She gave it up, fell back on the old one, maybe the oldest one of all: "Lord have mercy. Lord have mercy. Lord have mercy."

She was babbling like an idiot. The darkness laughed at her. She could not listen to it, or she would fail.

It struck like a snake, straight at her hand. She jerked back. The parchment crumbled. The living thread stretched. She stilled with an effort that shook her nearly out of her seat.

Too late. The thread snapped. The world cracked open and flung her down and down and down.

Rowan woke up with a hideous headache. She was lying on something hard and knobby, not like her bed at all. It moved, cursing in very bad Greek.

Then it spoke in decent Frankish with a Breton lilt. "Your elbow is embedded in my liver. Do you mind . . .?"

Rowan was too sore to mind. She moved her elbow. The rest of her slipped and came to ground with a thump, not a very hard one but enough to half blind her with the headache. It was a while before she could move again, or say anything that made sense.

Memory came back too soon. "Father! Where's—what—"

"He's breathing," said Kerrec. "I hear him."

So, too painfully, could Rowan. It was regular, even, the breathing of a man deep asleep. Nothing unusual in it. Nothing at all, anywhere, to show that a great sorcery had come and gone, and knocked two witch-children flat.

Except for one thing. It was a little thing, a harmless thing, but in Rowan's weakened condition it loomed enormous. The Emperor's snoring had stopped.

Nine

· · · · · · · · · · · · ·

*T*HE EMPEROR WAS UP in the morning, doing as he always did, seeming as hearty as he always was, eating his breakfast and receiving the first of the day's audiences and swimming in the baths. But if the Emperor seemed well enough, Rowan was not. Her headache would not go away, and the rest of her ached almost as much. Still, she stayed stubbornly near him. People thought him excessively affectionate toward his daughters, and far too indulgent in keeping them so close about him, but for once it served Rowan well. Kerrec had not been able to stay; he had the Elephant to look after, and that duty he would not shirk.

Toward midmorning, fresh and ruddy from his bath, the Emperor decided to go hunting. A boar had been vexing one of the villages, and the villagers had sent a deputation to beg the Emperor's help in getting rid of the beast. "Roast boar for dinner!" the Emperor said in high glee, shouting for his horse and his huntsmen.

And what, thought Rowan, if this was the barb of

the spell? Boars were the devil's beast, cunning and murderous. What if this boar was set to kill the Emperor?

As he strode out of the audience chamber, she set herself in his way. "Father, won't you let it wait for a while?"

He kept on striding, sweeping her in his wake. "And why should I let it wait?" he asked her. "We haven't had roast boar in an age. Aren't you hungry for a platterful?"

"I think you should wait," she said. "Maybe someone else will kill it for you."

That was a mistake. He paused in midstride. His frank open face had gone dark with anger. "Are you saying I'm too old to hunt boar?"

"No!" she cried. "*No*, Father. I just don't—Oh!" She blurted it out all at once, and never mind the consequences. "What if it kills you?"

"There," he said, growing easy again. "There, little bird. I can't say it won't happen, but how many years have I gone out on the hunt and come back without a scratch?"

"Today is different," said Rowan. "I know it."

"There, there," said the Emperor. He was not listening to her at all.

Rowan rode with the hunt. On any other day she would have loved the spectacle of it, all the hunters mounted and afoot, the great boarhounds baying, the forest in its summer green, misted still in the hollows, and a soft grey haze on the sun's face. They began in a pack, with Rowan not far from the lead on swift Galla, as near her father as she could be. He had a helmet on, and his old leather coat, and a bundle of boar-spears strapped to his saddle; he was singing in his high voice, pausing to laugh at something somebody said. There were many dressed more brightly or more richly, and some who had a better seat on a horse, but to Rowan's eye there was no mistaking what he was. He carried himself like a man who ruled the world.

She loved him so much that it hurt, and she wanted to drag him down off his horse and shake him till he listened to her. She did not know what she would do if the boar tried to kill him. Be a martyr, probably, fling herself in front of it and give her father time to get away.

They started animals enough as they ran the wood: rabbits, deer, something enormous and snorting that the huntsmen said was not a boar but an aurochs, a bull of the woods. Rowan had a moment of exquisite horror, of certainty that the beast was a demon. But it crashed away into the deep cover and did not come back.

Some of the younger lords went yelling after it. Rowan stayed with her father. One or two people muttered about that. The Emperor stopped them with a look. His daughters, it said, had always gone where they wished to go. And they knew well enough to get out of the way when the men needed room to work.

They were a good league out of Aachen now, on a track that ran north from the village that had lost one of its children to the boar. "Ate him," the woman in the delegation had said in a hard dry voice, as if she was burned empty of tears. "Flung him down and tusked him to pieces and devoured his entrails. That's not boar's work, sire, boar's tusks or no. That's a devil out of the black places."

"Boar will go rogue sometimes," the Emperor had said, "which is ill for you and yours. We'll get him for you, good wife. Have no fear of it."

It would have been proper for the woman to fall weeping at his feet, babbling thanks, but she was not that kind of woman. She ducked in a sort of curtsy, pulled her companions together with a glance, and left without a word. Whether she believed the Emperor or simply had been trying a last resort, Rowan still, half a day later, could not tell.

They had ridden through the woman's village but not paused in it. It was small, poor but clean, with a sow in a wallow by the well, suckling a wriggling mass of piglets. Rowan thought the piglets looked rather rangy and dark. Maybe the boar was not a devil after all. Maybe he had been coming to visit the sow, and the child had got in his way, and somehow made him angry. Children could do that. They were very good at it.

But she was no less desperately uneasy. She had not dreamed what she saw in the night. She knew that as well as she knew anything. There was a sorcery on her father. Soon or late, it was going to strike.

At least her headache was gone. The clean air and the fast pace had swept it away. Galla had stopped throwing her head against the bit as she did when she wanted to punish Rowan for not riding enough, and settled down to a level pace.

The noisy idiots who had gone after the aurochs came back as noisy as ever, but their horses were blown; they whooped and shouted at the back of the hunt, where they had to work harder to annoy Rowan. The hounds had gone quiet except for an occasional yip. Rowan ducked under a branch and thought about slowing Galla down for a bit, to let her get her breath. Her father's big grey was dark with sweat but going steady.

The quiet shattered with the clamor of hounds.

Rowan knew the song of boarhounds on boar. So did everyone else. Horns brayed. Men hallooed.

The chase was on.

The Emperor and his men hunted the boar through the tangled wood. Rowan hunted the Emperor. At length the wood grew so tangled that horses could not run; the hunters dismounted and left the horses with the servants and a few disgruntled squires, and pushed on afoot.

Rowan was not a sedentary lady. She rode her pony, she walked in Aachen and about the palace, she was not so many months past hoydening in the woods. But this was a run to leave even a trained warrior winded and staggering: beating through brush and briars, leaping fallen trees, catching skirt or sleeve on branches or thorns. Some of the hunters had shed their cloaks to run easier. Rowan paused briefly to do the same, and to kilt her skirts up higher. She had trews on underneath, which was fortunate. The brambles were fierce.

Her father was still in sight, his helmet bobbing and ducking through the wood, up a slope and down again, and over a trickle of stream. One or two people stopped to drink, but Rowan pressed on, because her father did. He was not a graceful runner, and when he was tired he limped from an old wound, but he was fast enough for that, and he never seemed to tire.

It was a small gratification to see how redfaced and breathless the men about her were becoming, and how more of them fell back, the farther they went. The ones who stayed in the race were the huntsmen, who were used to running on foot, and the most stubborn of the noblemen, and the Emperor's squire. And Rowan, who was so dizzy with exhaustion that she did not even feel it any longer.

She had been running forever. She would run forever. Over this log, round this tree, through this knot of brambles. The hounds had changed their song again. This deep-throated bellow meant that they had the boar at bay. She heard its snorting, and a shrill squeal followed by the yelp of a hound in pain.

She had to catch her father before he reached the boar—she knew that in her bones. She had to stop him, let another make the kill. But he was a whole furlong ahead of her, as far away as the moon, and as uncatchable.

Then he was right in front of her, and she crashed into him. Her feet could not stop running. Her lungs could not find air. He staggered but did not go down, half-whirling, his eyes vivid with anger, till he saw who it was. Rowan clung to him and gasped.

Through the darkness that came and went in front of her eyes, she saw what had made him stop: a clearing, and at its end a wall of stone, and at the foot of the wall a milling, howling, battling half-circle of hounds, and in the center of the half-circle, the boar.

The wall was a crag with water running down it, too little to be reckoned a waterfall. The boar's absurdly tiny hoofs churned the mud of the base. The hounds, white and red and brown, were speckled black with mud. One or two had leaped in too close: their sides were stained scarlet. The boar's eye seemed redder yet. It glared at the hounds, the hunt, the world that had betrayed it and would drive it to its death.

No boar ever went alone into the dark, if it could help it. This one slashed at a dog that sprang for its hamstrings. Rowan saw the white tusk pierce the brindled side, saw it catch and tear, and the dog go flying, trailing blood and entrails.

Her father pried her arms loose from about his middle. He said something; she thought it might have been, "Stay here," and advanced on the boar. His spear was leveled, its bronze head gleaming darkly.

There were others moving in, but they gave place to the Emperor. A few were laughing as men will when they fight. Most were silent, intent. No raw boys had come this far, at this speed. These all knew how great the danger was, how deadly fast a boar could be, how terribly strong.

Rowan had no spear. She had never been taught to use one. She had to stand helpless as she too often did, and for once she was not inclined to pray. Prayer had not stopped Michael Phokias. Why would it stop a maddened boar?

Guilt stabbed her. She said a quick *Gloria Patri*, never taking her eyes from her father.

He advanced without haste, seeming to ponder each step before he took it. At just the right point, outside the circle of dogs and in the direct path of the boar's escape, he dropped on one knee and braced his heavy spear in the ground and nodded to the huntsmen. They dived into the pack of dogs, hauling them off, whipping and cursing and making a deafening din.

The boar was occupied with the innermost circle of hounds, the best and the bravest, who harried it mercilessly while the pups and the lesser dogs dropped away. When there was no circle but the inner, the master huntsman lashed the flank of a spotted bitch. She turned on him; he leaped back. The boar saw the opening and charged.

It hurtled straight out of the circle, straight at the Emperor. All that was between him and tusked death was the blade of his spear, and its shaft, and the guard a bare arm's length from his hand. The boar was mad with rage, its flank torn by a flashing strike as it passed the spotted bitch, its tusks red with hounds' blood. It flung itself full on the spear, driving up and up it, slashing, squealing, snapping in the Emperor's face.

The spear rocked, and slipped in the soft earth. The boar fought its death, twisting on the shaft that impaled it. Only the iron crosspiece held it, and the Emperor's strength. He seemed rooted in the earth, swaying like a tree in a gale. But he was holding; meeting the boar eye to reddened eye.

The boar died in pieces like the hound it had killed. First its hindquarters went limp, then its scrabbling forefeet, then its jaws opening, closing, its head twisting to slash at its own pain, its eyes filming over, the whole heavy body sagging against the shaft of the spear.

The Emperor held for a while after the boar was dead, to be sure of it. When it was completely still, he drew back carefully. His squire sprang in to brace the spear, in case the boar revived before the huntsmen could make sure of it. The Emperor straightened, a little stiff, but grinning like a boy.

One of the lords sent up a shout. *"Montjoie!"*

"Montjoie!" the others echoed him, exultant. *"Montjoie! Montjoie! Montjoie!"* And over and under and around it: "Carl! Carl! Carl! Carl!"

Carl the Emperor took the cheers, like the victory, as his due. He gutted the boar with his own hands and gave the dogs their tribute, and left the rest of the butchering to the huntsmen. And all the while he smiled, delighted with himself and his world.

Rowan was smiling, too. She could hardly help it. The boar was thoroughly and inarguably dead. Her father was as thoroughly alive. They all came out of the thickets singing, with the boar trussed to a pole and a pair of brawny lads carrying it, to find the horses and the stragglers all gathered under the trees. The Emperor had stopped at the stream to wash the blood from his face and hands, but it stained his coat still, his badge of honor from the hunt.

He bade Rowan ride beside him on the way back. She was glad to do that, though she was feeling ill again.

The scent of the boar's blood seemed to wreathe every-thing, thick and cloying. She was having trouble seeing clearly. The Emperor seemed to be wearing a chain about his neck, a narrow strand of silver so tarnished it was black. But he owned no such chain, and no jewel to sus-pend from it. It was a trick of the light, or of the way his coat was fastened. Or maybe the boar's blood had sprayed and darkened, and seemed to circle his throat.

But when she blinked, it did not go away. And when they came out of the forest's dimness into a day still fully light, and showed the boar's carcass to the villagers, he had the mark still, or the chain, or whatever it was. She was afraid to call it what it must be: the sorcerer's spell made somehow visible, maybe because she was too tired not to see it.

The villagers were glad in a dour way. The slain child's mother said nothing. She stared at the boar as if to commit it to memory, and her face wore no more expression than it ever had.

"Good wife," said the Emperor, "would you be want-ing to take this as the wergild for your son?"

The woman seemed not to hear him at first. Then she shook herself hard, so hard Rowan heard her teeth click together. "No," she said, or Rowan thought she said, indistinctly. And louder: "No. Take it and eat it. We won't touch flesh that ate our son's flesh."

Some of the hunters looked queasy at the thought, but the Emperor inclined his head. "As you wish. Good day to you, and God's blessing on you and the rest of your sons."

"I have no more sons," said the woman. She stood

97

like a tree as they rode away, eyes fixed on the ground where the boar had lain, where its blood had seeped into the earth.

When they were out of sight of the village, the Emperor shook his head. "There's a sad grim creature," he said.

"Maybe she'll come out of her grief now the boar is dead," said Rowan.

"Maybe," said the Emperor.

She could see that he did not believe it. Nor, much, did she. People who grieved could do strange things, but this woman looked as if she had been born grieving.

Well, thought Rowan. The boar was dead, and would kill no more children. "Father," she said, "will you eat the boar tonight?"

He raised his brows. "So you think she was right?"

"I don't know," said Rowan. "It's just . . . what if it lived on manflesh?"

"Oh, I doubt that," he said. "Its entrails were full of beechmast and acorns—good boar sausage, and no meat that we could see."

"Then maybe it's not the boar that killed the boy."

The Emperor laughed, which almost made her angry. But he was not laughing at her, not really. "Then we'll have to go hunting again. But I think it was the right one. Adalbold is a very good tracker, and he says that this is the boar that left spoor in the village."

"I hope so," said Rowan, crossing herself to make it surer. The Emperor's neck seemed clear now of marks or scars. She had been tired, that was all, and worn out with being afraid for him.

A little farther on, the road was wider and clearer. Some of the younger men, seeing that the Emperor was inclined to be lenient, surged round him. The Emperor's stallion fretted and bucked. He laughed and let it go.

Rowan was almost caught behind, but Galla was never one to miss a race. She leaped from sedate trot into flying gallop.

They ran past fear, past grief, past anything at all but the glory of speed. The grey stallion was just ahead, taunting Galla with his heels. She set her head and pinned her ears and showed him what she thought of that. Her mane whipped Rowan's hands. Her back surged and sank, surged and sank. Her hoofs thudded on the packed earth. The stallion's rump was level with Galla's nose, then her neck, then her shoulder.

Carl turned his head. He was laughing. He leaned forward over his horse's neck, urging it on. But Galla was having none of it. They were neck and neck now, grey stallion, bay mare.

It happened very slowly. Rowan did not even know what she was seeing till afterward. It seemed that the chain about the Emperor's neck thickened to a cord, and from a cord to a rope. And drew suddenly tight.

One moment he was racing, laughing, urging his stallion to outrun that upstart of a mare. The next, he was falling, tumbling slowly like a juggler at a fair, arms and legs like the spokes of a wheel, horse vanishing from beneath him, earth rising to meet him.

Rowan had no memory of reining Galla to a halt, hauling her round, sending her plunging back toward the man on the ground. But Rowan was there, still mounted, and he was there, still fallen, and she knew nothing, not even whether he was alive or dead.

Ten

. . . .

THE EMPEROR WAS ALIVE. That was all, at first, that Rowan cared for. But alive was not enough. He could not ride or walk or talk. He had to be carried back to Aachen, mute and staring, with such a look of shock in his eyes that Rowan wanted to howl.

They thought he had had an apoplexy. His doctors discoursed learnedly on its causes and effects, and debated endless treatments, each more preposterous than the last. They had the Emperor in their power at last, who had always mocked and scorned them, and they were taking full advantage of it.

Someone else drove them out before Rowan could, with as much sheer rampant gusto as the Emperor ever had. And well she might: the Abbess Gisela was great Carl's sister. She did not look so very much like him, slender silvery creature that she was, like the niece who was named after her, but she had her brother's sharp wit and his strength of will. Rowan, seeing her, burst into tears.

"There now," said the abbess when the last of the

doctors had fled in a flapping of robes, and the servants were left to look after the Emperor in peace. "Suppose you tell me what happened to him."

Rowan tried to take in a breath. It turned to a hiccough, and then to a strangled shriek. The abbess set her down briskly in a chair and poured unwatered wine into her until she stopped sobbing and gulped. The wine burned as it went down. The fumes rose at once to her head. Oddly, they steadied her.

"Now," said the abbess. "What's so bad that you can't tell me?"

Rowan found words to say, and breath to say them with. "I can't tell you."

"Then what good is it?" the abbess inquired.

Rowan stared at her. There was little else she could do, with the abbess' hand cupping her chin and the abbess' face filling her vision. The younger Gisela would look like this, if she lived so long: her silver-gilt gone to silver, her beauty thinned and fined with fasting till it shone out of her like light from a lamp. But Gisela's eyes would never be as keen as these, or as pitiless.

"Aunt," said Rowan with a small sigh, maybe of despair, maybe of relief, "if I told you, you'd tell me I was vaporing."

"Tell me," said the Abbess Gisela.

This brisk good sense was what Rowan had run away to find, when her magic was still so new that she could not endure it. Kerrec and the Elephant had prevented her then. They were nowhere in evidence now. *Deserters*, a small part of Rowan muttered. The rest of her looked for

102

a way to put everything into words that her aunt would listen to, and understand.

There was no way, really, but to tell it straight out. "There's a sorcery on him," said Rowan.

The abbess' eyes narrowed, but she did not say anything, only waited for Rowan to go on.

Rowan had more than half hoped for a reprieve. She should have known better. She breathed deep. This time it did not break into sobbing. She told the whole thing then, from the beginning, the day the Elephant came to Aachen.

When she was done, her throat was sore with talking, and her head was aching all over again. The abbess had not spoken through any of it, or changed expression, or done anything but listen. At the end of it she nodded slowly. "I knew it would come to this," she said as if to herself.

"To what?" Rowan asked before she thought.

"You," said the abbess. "This. Your mother was not well loved, and for good reason. She was never precisely tactful about what she was."

"She wasn't a witch!"

Rowan had said it so often that it was like a ritual. The abbess knew that very well, but still she chose to answer it. "She was something other than a simple woman, then, whatever you want to call her. She saw things that no one else could see. She could bend a man to her will with a look—"

"So can any beautiful woman," said Rowan.

"She wasn't beautiful," the abbess said. "Not that it

mattered. She had lineage and lands and the art of pleasing a man, and her ambition was charming when she was young. She never worked her will on my brother, that's true, unless he wished her to. He married her of his own free will, knowing what he had, and rather more proud of it than not."

"She didn't lay a spell on him," Rowan said, drawing herself into a knot of misery. "She *didn't*."

"She didn't need to," the abbess said.

Rowan glanced toward the bed. The Emperor was laid in it, washed, clothed in a clean white shirt and covered with a light silken coverlet. He had not moved through washing or tending or dressing, except, once in a great while, to close his eyes, then to open them again. He was closing them more often now than he opened them. "Do you believe me?" she asked her aunt.

The abbess did not answer at once. She was staring at the Emperor, too. There was no telling what she thought. "It might be wise," she said after a while, "to let people think that he's taken sick as old men do. An apoplexy is thoroughly credible in a man of his girth and habits."

"Why?" Rowan demanded. "Why don't we tell everybody? Then they'll drive the sorcerer out."

"Do you want them to? Think, child. We know where the Greek is, and what he does. If he's driven out, who knows where he'll go, or what vengeance he'll take?"

Rowan did not want to yield to the sense of that, but she had learned long ago not to argue with the abbess when she wore that particular, forbidding expression.

"And," said the abbess, "we know something that

the Greeks aren't aware we know. Everybody here thinks that they speak for the Empress. We know that she was deposed and is dead, and that an emperor rules in her place."

"If I didn't dream it all," said Rowan, "or let the Breton deceive me."

"I doubt he did," the abbess said. "You're not an easy person to deceive, except when you're trying to deceive yourself."

That was hardly fair, in Rowan's opinion. The abbess had got up from beside Rowan's chair and gone to stand by the bed. She shook her head, looking down at her brother. "Ah, Carl, if I could disbelieve her, I'd be a happier woman."

"But what can we do?" Rowan cried.

"We'll think of something," the abbess said. "Go on now. Young things need to eat, and you need sleep."

"I don't want to leave him," said Rowan stubbornly. "Who will protect him them?"

"You don't think I can do it?"

Rowan met those clear pale eyes and shivered. She would not have wagered on the devil himself to face down the Abbess Gisela. "If you'd been here last night . . ." she began.

"If I'd been here last night, I would have been praying in the chapel, and doing no good at all. Now, Theoderada. Supper. Then bed."

No one else could have taken that tone with Rowan and been listened to. But Aunt Gisela had been afflicting Rowan with her merciless good sense since Rowan was a weanling. There was nothing for it but to give in to it, whether she wanted to or no.

Rowan ate, somewhat to her surprise, and slept, to her lasting astonishment. Bertrada did not come to bed that Rowan knew of, and if the maid snored, Rowan was oblivious. She did not even dream, that she remembered.

She woke in the grey dawn with an ache in her throat that spoke of tears, and the salt taste of them on her tongue. For a blessed moment she could not remember why she might have been crying in her sleep. Then it all flooded back.

She got up, washed and dressed herself and plaited her hair, and said her prayers. No one else was awake in the women's palace, although the cooks were in the kitchens: she smelled the incomparable smell of new bread baking.

The morning was heavy with mist, the air chill. Rowan was glad she had thought to put on her mantle. She picked her way across a dew-wet courtyard, slipping on the stones that paved it, and cut through a corner of the garden. Her shoes were soaking by the time she came to the menagerie's gate.

The menagerie was an eerie place in that light. Cages loomed grey out of the mist; the creatures in them slept, dark huddled shapes in corners, or stared at her with lambent eyes. Something shrieked like a damned soul. Rowan nigh jumped out of her skin, but it was only a peacock waking out of sorts, pecking the nearest of his hens and dragging his tail behind him as he went in search of breakfast. Rowan had not thought to bring anything for him. It was one more misery to add to the rest, small amid everything else, but weighty for its size.

The door to the Elephant's house was shut this morning. Rowan slipped through the small one set inside it.

The odor of elephant swept over her. There was light, surprisingly bright, from louvers in the roof, and from tall windows too narrow to let the Elephant escape. It shone on the mountain of hay that had been brought in yesterday, and the gilded howdah, and the chest where the rest of the Elephant's trappings were kept. The Elephant was farther in, in his stall, blending so well with the shadows that for a moment Rowan thought his tusks were tricks of the light.

Then he came clear, all the vast grey bulk of him, and the smaller shadow that was his keeper, leaning against his foreleg. Kerrec looked as if he had not slept in longer than Rowan had.

"And where were you," she demanded, knowing it was unjust but refusing to care, "when the sorcerer trapped my father?"

"Abul Abbas is ill," said Kerrec as if she had not spoken.

"My father might die," Rowan said, "and you were hiding here, behind an elephant."

Then his words caught up with her. "Ill?" She peered. The Elephant was unusually still. He had not stretched out his trunk to her as he usually did, or looked at her, or seemed aware that there was anyone with him at all.

In the pause he sighed, a sound like wind in the rafters, and nosed listlessly at the mound of hay in front of him.

"He hasn't eaten in two days," Kerrec said. "He won't tell me what's wrong."

"Maybe it's grief still," said Rowan. "Or maybe he ate something that disagreed with him."

Kerrec's lip curled. "If it were that simple, do you think I wouldn't know it?"

"How do I know what anybody knows of elephants? Maybe he's tied to the Talisman," Rowan said. "Maybe he can't tell you because there's a spell on him, too."

She was only letting her fancy run wild, but Kerrec seized on it with ferocity that took her aback. "Yes, I thought of that. I'd be almost sure of it, if he'd only *tell* me."

"Why does he need to tell you? He's an animal. Animals don't use words."

"You don't care about him at all," said Kerrec angrily. "You don't care if he lives or dies."

"I care if my father dies," Rowan shot back, "which is more than you ever did."

Kerrec's jaw set. He shook his head, not to deny what she said, not exactly; more as if he was weary of the whole fruitless argument. "Nothing we do seems to help anything. Mostly we just make it worse."

Rowan snorted in disgust. "Now you're going all over Breton again, gloom and doom and black despair. That's not doing us any good at all."

"You're a cold hard creature, do you know that? Your father's dying. Why aren't you at his bedside?"

"Because that's not where I can help him." Rowan would not break down and cry in front of Kerrec, however badly she wanted to. She moved closer, looking up at the motionless bulk of the Elephant. His hide was as soft to the touch as ever, and maybe a little warmer, but not warm enough for fever. His trunk hung slack; his eye was dull. His ears did not even flick to dislodge the flies.

She brushed them away, as high as she could reach. She might have been invisible, for all the notice he took of her. Her throat hurt. Somehow it was harder to keep from crying over the Elephant than over her father. They had the same mute passivity, the same utter unlikeness to themselves, but the man had all the help any living thing could have. The Elephant had nothing but Kerrec, and Rowan. No one else knew enough to care.

"You're arrogant, you know," said Kerrec, "to think that you can be of any help to your father. That's a task for priests and princes."

"And wizards of the Bretons?"

She was mocking him, and he could not help but know it. His eyes glittered. "The great ones never leave their native earth. Here, there's only I, and I'm too weak to fight this magic."

She could dispute it till she was breathless, but there was no doubt of the truth. "Then we have no help and no hope, and we can only wait for both of them to die." She stiffened her back. "I don't care how true that is. I won't accept it. Somehow — some way —"

"Stubborn," said Kerrec, who was no sweet yielding flower himself.

"I'll be anything I have to be," said Rowan, "to keep my father alive."

"Even a witch?"

She went rigid.

"You can't go that far, can you?" Kerrec said. "You can't really do it."

"I'll prove I can."

"How?"

Rowan had no words to say, though she hunted for any that would do. Kerrec, who should have laughed in her face, sank down with his back against the treetrunk solidity of the Elephant's foot. "I think I'm tired of despair," he said. "I know I'm tired of thinking I can save everything if I only knew how. What if both of them did die? Maybe it's their time."

"God would never use that devil's sorcery," Rowan said fiercely.

"Why? Do you share his secrets?"

She could hit him. That would feel wonderful. She could run away from him. That would be prudent. She chose instead to sit on her heels in front of him, skirts tucked about her, and glare at him until a faint flush stained his cheeks under their olive-brownness. "Can you think of anything at all useful to do or say?" she asked him mildly, under the circumstances.

"No," said Kerrec.

Rowan sighed. Tears were farther away than they had been for a while. The knot of misery was still there in her center, but she could think around it. "Neither can I," she said. "But I will. While I wait—" She paused.

Her shoulders were stiff; her hands were damp and cold. "Will you teach me? To use magic?"

"No," said Kerrec.

Rowan reared back till she almost fell over. "What do you mean, 'No'? Who else in Aachen can teach me?"

"No one," he said.

"Then why—"

"Because I don't know everything that I should know, and what I do know is man's magic, and you are a woman; your magic is different. Because if I teach you what little I do know, and if it helps you at all, who's to say I won't be caught and flogged for tempting the Emperor's daughter into iniquity?"

"Then you're a worse coward than I am," Rowan said bitterly. "You won't even try."

He laughed, flat and hard. "You don't know what it is to be anything but a princess. Whatever your father allows, you can do; if he's difficult, you wheedle him round. The rest of the world has to live by other laws. It's not your back that would be laid open if we were caught, or your life that would hang in the balance if our crime were reckoned great enough. The worst that you would suffer would be confinement to a convent for a while—and you would find that more restful than not."

"That's not so," said Rowan.

"Of course it's so," said Kerrec. "You don't want to see it, that's all. You are safe no matter what I do. I pay whatever penalty we both deserve."

"No," said Rowan.

He shrugged, so arrogant and so indifferent that she

hated him. "If you can't face that, how do you expect to face magic?"

"I faced it when the Greek took the Talisman."

"You faced dire necessity. Now the worst is done. We lost that fight. Victory now, or even stalemate, will be long and slow and deadly uncertain. How much courage do you have, king's daughter? How much strength is in you?"

"More than you would ever admit," said Rowan.

"Then teach yourself magic."

"But I *can't!*"

"Then don't," said Kerrec. He drew up his knees and clasped them, letting his head droop over them. She could see his face still. It was closed tight.

Rowan despised every bit of him, right down to the patch in his shoe. Damnable, prickly, unreasonable sprat of a Breton. How dared he speak so to her? She was the Emperor's daughter. He was no one at all.

The Elephant shifted slightly, curled his trunk and uncurled it, and sighed. Rowan's anger melted in fear for him, for her father, for everything she knew. Even for Kerrec.

"I don't know why I trouble myself with you," she said out of the last of her temper. "You're all edges, like a rackful of knives. Don't you cut yourself, with so many?"

"All the time," said Kerrec. Neither tone nor face showed any sign of softening, but he had answered her. That was enough.

She had known horses like him. Stallions, usually, too young to know what they wanted, but old enough to

112

be outspoken about it. The good ones steadied as they grew. Kerrec would steady, she thought. If he lived that long.

"If you won't teach me," she said with care, "would you stay by me while I learn, and stop me if I stumble?"

"Do you trust me to do that?"

"Who else is there to trust?"

"Why, no one," he said. "No one in the world."

Eleven

*R*OWAN HAD CROSSED a line, that early morning in the Elephant's house. The full force of it did not strike her for a long while after; by then it was too late to turn back.

Using magic to stop a spell in the working was one thing. She had had to do that. Using it in cold blood, with intent to make it stronger, was another thing altogether. And surely it was proof that she was damned.

She wondered if her sisters felt the same way when they took their lovers, knowing that it was a sin, but unable to stop.

"Nonsense," said Kerrec, to whom she let the thought slip. "Taking lovers doesn't offer some hope of keeping an emperor alive."

"How do we know that?" Rowan asked. Kerrec did not dignify it with an answer.

With the Emperor's illness, everything seemed to stop. The life of the palace went on, that was true. People had to eat, sleep, go about their business. The city was as crowded as ever, the churches full of prayers and incense. But the heart of it was a man mute and all but lifeless in a bed, and the silence of those who kept vigil, and the doctors' muttering.

To Rowan it felt like the stillness before a storm's breaking. She did not see the Byzantines anywhere, would have thought them sensible if they had made excuses and left, but they were still in Aachen. There was no mistaking that sensation of rats in the rafters. Michael Phokias would not leave until he had proof of his victory.

She spent a great deal of time with the Elephant, and coincidentally with Kerrec. But she could not sleep there, as safe as she knew it would be. People were talking enough already about the time she spent with the Elephant—and the Elephant's boy.

The Elephant, like the Emperor, had sunk into silence. Sometimes Kerrec could coax him to eat a mouthful, or to go out into the sun. Mostly the great beast stood unmoving in his stall. Day by day his skin seemed more wrinkled, the arch of his back more distinct. His ribs were like the ribs of a ship Rowan had seen once careened on the sand at Brundisium, when she went with her father to Italy.

Her father was sturdier, or his frame less susceptible to the ravages of sickness. He looked as solid as ever under his coverlet. But his face had lost its ruddy glow, and his hands folded on his breast were suddenly an old man's hands, rope-veined and sharp-boned and frail.

The great chapel was full of people praying for the Emperor. The women's chapel had a priest in it, saying

Mass. Rowan's sisters were there, all but Hrotrud, who was not diligent in her devotions. Rowan saw Gisela's silver-gold head beside Bertha's wheat-gold one, and one in a veil beyond them, keen eyes lowered, white still-beautiful face rapt in prayer.

Rowan had not been going to go in, but she found herself beside her aunt, close enough to the younger Gisela and far enough to the side to see her face. That was as lovely as always, and no more vapid than usual, fixed on the priest as he moved through the Mass.

And yet cold walked down Rowan's spine. She had been too intent on her own troubles to take much notice of Gisela now that the Talisman was in another's hands. If she had thought of her sister at all, she had thought that, once he was done with her, Michael Phokias would have let her go. He could hardly kill her to keep her quiet. Too many people would notice.

Something was not right with Gisela. It was nothing that the eye could see or the mind catch hold of. It was more like a prickle in the back of the skull, a quiver in the thing that Rowan had learned to call her magic.

The Mass crawled to its end. Everyone lingered to pray. Rowan prayed, she had reason enough. She hoped that God was as capacious as the priests said, or she would overburden him with all the things she needed him to look after.

The Abbess Gisela was one of the first to leave. Princess Gisela was one of the last. When at great length Gisela rose from her knees and crossed herself three times, bowing to the altar, Rowan got up a shade more slowly and with fewer gestures, eyes fixed on her sister. Gisela seemed not to notice her, even when she went out right on Gisela's heels.

Rowan should probably have tried for concealment, but the same instinct that cried warning about Gisela cried none about secrecy. So she took the easier way, walking behind her sister, following where she went.

It was not very interesting. She went to the gallery first, and stitched at the altar cloth she had been stitching at for the last month and more. Her stitches were as even as ever, her embroidery as exquisite. She did not say anything to the others, but then no one was saying much.

After a while she got up. Again Rowan got up to follow her. She caught a sharp glance from her aunt, but no one else seemed to notice.

This time Gisela went outside. It was nowhere incriminating, only the herb garden. She wandered aimlessly, with Rowan for a shadow. Once she plucked a sprig of rosemary and held it to her nose. For a moment something changed, as if the old Gisela woke and wondered where she was; then the rosemary dropped from her fingers and she wandered on.

"And that's all she did," Rowan said to Kerrec. "Wandered. Sniffed the flowers. Sat in the sun and folded her hands in her lap, and there she stayed till dinnertime, and not a word out of her."

Kerrec had been eating his own dinner when Rowan found him. She had had no appetite for hers. She took the bread he offered, hardly noticing what it was, and bit into it just as absently.

"You should have steered her into the rosemary bush," Kerrec said. "Then maybe she would have remembered."

Rowan bridled a little. "Why on earth should I have done that?"

"Rosemary's a healing herb," he said with such patience that she could have hit him. "It helps the memory."

"But what could she have forgotten?"

He looked at her as if she had forgotten her wits. "What could she have remembered? She had the Talisman for long enough to make it her own, even if she didn't know what she was doing. Then she gave it up. Look at what happened to your father, and to Abul Abbas. How could she keep from catching the edge of the spell?"

"But she's an innocent," said Rowan. "She never knew what she had."

"Nor did your father. And what is Abul Abbas but an innocent?"

"Abul Abbas is as wise as Solomon. He knows much more than he's telling."

Kerrec granted the truth of that, no more graciously than he ever did. "That's three whom the spell has touched. We say in Brittany that there's power in threes. What kind of power would a sorcerer want from an emperor and a princess and an elephant?"

"From the Emperor, it's obvious," Rowan said. "From the princess, too."

"She's not the only daughter," said Kerrec.

"But Bertha is protected," Rowan said. "She's as good as married to Father Angilbert, and everybody knows it. Hrotrud will marry nobody, and she's too fierce to be tamed as Gisela was. The rest of us are younger, and negligible."

"Then why the Elephant?"

"Because he's part of the Talisman. Because he's exotic, and strange, and prized by the Emperor. Or maybe," said Rowan, "that was an accident, and so was Gisela. All he really wanted was my father."

She could say it steadily, think it clearly. She had had enough time to steel herself to it. But inside she kept wanting to break down and howl.

Kerrec stroked the Elephant's trunk gently, as he had been doing off and on since this bleak conversation began. Maybe he thought that it helped, somehow, if only to make him feel that he was doing something.

"Do you think," Rowan asked him, "that rosemary would make Gisela remember? Would it help Father, too? We could roast a lamb in it, feed it to them both."

Hope rose as she spoke, and got into her voice. Kerrec dashed it. "If it were only a spell of forgetfulness — yes, it would help, a little. But this is a great working, with a demon in it. He'd only laugh at your little banners of herbs."

"Maybe little things are better than great things, for this," said Rowan stubbornly.

"No," said Kerrec, just as stubborn.

Rowan scrambled up from where she had been

sitting in the Elephant's uneaten hay. "I'll try it in spite of you. It's better than sitting here feeling sorry for myself."

The Emperor's master cook was an awesome personage, a great prince of his kind and mightily aware of it, but he had always been indulgent with Rowan. Mostly it was because she liked to watch him work, but she knew how to keep quiet, and she had not prattled about his secrets even when she was small and given to telling everything she knew. And then she was good at tasting for him—she could tell if something needed seasoning, if not always exactly what. He had said once where she could hear, that it was unfortunate she was a girl and a princess; she would have made a decent cook.

Of course Master Gottfried would never say it to her face. He was as intent on his work as an emperor in a battle, and as caught up in marshaling his forces. A palace needed an army of cooks and undercooks and apprentice cooks, scullions and spitboys and potboys, bread-bakers and meat-carvers and hearth-tenders, and one haughty personage whose chief task was to mete out the spices from their hoard. The master cook oversaw them all. He had a chair where he could see the whole kitchen, but he was never in it. He was always in the thick of things.

This evening Rowan found him at the spits. They were roasting an ox whole, and one of the chains had given way. The fire had been doused, at what cost in curses Rowan could well guess, and a pair of brawny scullions stood in the still-smoking embers, struggling to restore the chain. A third, much smaller boy poured water over their leather-booted feet, with much hissing and bellowing of steam.

It was very like the hell the priest had droned about at Mass. Rowan wished she could consign Michael Phokias to it, and quickly; but wishing was no way to work real magic, as she had already learned to her sorrow.

Master Gottfried had no time to greet her, even if she had expected any such thing. She stayed quiet and out of the way while he saw the spit repaired and the fire rebuilt and the ox returned to its roasting. The only sign of impatience that she allowed herself was a shifting from foot to foot and a darting of glances about. The ox was just started; it would roast all night, slowly, till it was tender for tomorrow's dinner. Most of the cooks had gone, now that dinner was past, to take their well-earned ease. The scullions who scrubbed the pots were done, all but one who wore a look of martyrdom as he scoured the largest cauldron. One or two pots still simmered on the lesser hearth, with a yawning boy to oversee them. It was much too early for the bread-baking, much too late for the saucemaking.

In short, it was as quiet as the kitchen ever became, which was why Rowan had chosen this time to visit Master Gottfried. Once the spit was back in its place and the ox turning over the new-lit fire, he granted her the favor of a glance.

He was quite ordinary outside of the terror of his office, a middle-sized, mouse-colored man with a soft voice and a mild demeanor. He even smiled, sometimes, when he was not commanding his armies.

He did not smile now. No one did, since the Emperor had taken ill.

"Master," said Rowan forthrightly but with careful respect, "may I ask a favor of you?"

His eyebrows went up. Rowan was not given to asking favors, though she might wheedle the odd sweetcake out of him when his mood was amenable. "And what favor may that be?" he asked.

"Do you remember the broth you made once, that my father liked so well—the one with mutton in it, and barley? You put rosemary in it, with other herbs that made it really rather miraculous. And he ate it, though he never eats anything that isn't roasted or raw."

"He called it old man's gruel," said Master Gottfried, not without sharpness. "But yes, he ate it, and called for another bowl. We reckoned that a miracle here."

"We need another miracle," Rowan said. Her eyes pricked as they kept doing when she did not have Kerrec to stiffen her back for her. "I thought maybe, if you could tempt him—"

"It would take more than gruel to cure what ails him now," said Master Gottfried as gently as he ever said anything.

"He's not dying!"

The scullion with the cauldron had jumped right into it in startlement. They waited for the echoes to fade.

"He's ill," Rowan said more quietly, "but he's not going to die. Master Gottfried, will you make him your broth with the rosemary?"

"Rosemary to help him remember," said her father's master cook, shocking her speechless. "You think it will help, do you?"

Anyone else would have made her angry, talking to her like that. Master Gottfried honestly meant what he asked. "It could hardly hurt," she answered after a while. "And it might—just might—"

He did not think so, she could tell, but he nodded and went for his stockpot and his herbs. He was doing it for her father, and maybe a little for her. It was as much as he could do, and more than anyone else had done. Maybe he felt better for knowing that.

Rowan brought the bowl to her father with her own hands. His doctors had flocked back once Abbess Gisela was out of sight, but they were not allowed to do anything dangerous. There was no one else with him, except servants and his body-squire. Courtiers were being kept out, except those who had to be admitted, and those only for a little while.

She had had no more trouble with guards than she could easily put up with. The bowl was still warm in its shrouding of cloths when she set it on the table by the bed and uncovered it. The scent that wafted out made her mouth water.

The Emperor did not move. His eyes were nearly shut, a thin line of white showing, but no life or awareness.

With his squire's help she got him up and propped with bolsters. The boy had the same white, set expression she felt on her own face, the same rigidity that held back tears. "I'm not trying for miracles," she told him. "A single snore would do."

"What is this?" he asked. "Herb-healing?"

"Mutton stew," said Rowan.

"Same thing," he said.

Time was when she would have bristled, but that was before the world changed. She held the bowl under her father's nose. Nothing. Not a twitch.

He could eat if he was fed, she knew that already. He did it as a baby does, with as much dribbling, but he could swallow, and did, when he had to. She fed him half the bowl before he stopped swallowing. Then she waited. But she did not get her miracle, not even her snore. He was as empty as ever, like a man whose soul has gone wandering, leaving the body to fend for itself.

She had not been hoping. Not really. Just focusing on the action, and wanting it to help.

His squire laid him down again, wiped him clean, said nothing of blame or of disappointment. Rowan wished he would. Then she would have someone to rail at.

She would have been happy to fling the bowl out the window. She took it with her instead.

Gisela was in her bedchamber but not in her bed, sitting by the window as she had sat in the garden, with moonlight slanting on her face. She seemed to be drinking it.

Rowan held the bowl under her nose. She seemed as oblivious as the Emperor, but then, so suddenly Rowan started and almost dropped the bowl, her nose twitched.

The spoon was left behind in the Emperor's bedchamber. Rowan held the bowl to Gisela's lips. Gisela's hands came up to cover Rowan's.

She dashed the bowl in Rowan's face.

Rowan stood with broth and bits of mutton and barley and turnip and who knew what else running down her front. The odor of rosemary was strong, so strong that she gagged.

Gisela sat as she had before, motionless, with the moon pouring over her. She looked older just then than her aunt the abbess, as old as the moon, and as cold.

Twelve

· · · · · · · · · · · · ·

*H*ERBS ALONE could not heal a demon's work, Kerrec had said. "Drat and blast Kerrec," said Rowan to the Virgin in the chapel. Maybe to her mother, too.

"What do I do?" Rowan asked her. And then: "I know, I'm always asking that. But no one ever answers me."

Nor would her mother; or the Virgin. She had to find her own answers.

"Do I?" Rowan demanded. "Am I the one to do this, after all?"

She had asked that, too, more often than she could count. All the questions were the same ones, over and over. They never had answers.

"Maybe because there aren't any answers," Rowan said. "Maybe there's no hope. We aren't a nation of sorcerers. The Byzantines are. What defenses do we have against the likes of them?"

Some would say that piety was defense enough.

"Gisela would," said Rowan. "You see where it got her." She sighed. She was so tired she ached, but she seemed to have forgotten how to sleep. "Poor Gisela. She's not really stupid, you know. She's very good at astronomy. At anything, really, that she wants to bother with. She just doesn't want to bother with very much."

And maybe that was how the sorcerer had snared her. She cared for so little that was real; he had deluded her all the more easily for it.

"She's weak," said Rowan. "When anything's difficult, she gives up before she tries."

And yet, thought Rowan—and this time it really was Rowan, not that soft not-quite-voice in her head—was she herself any different?

She did not like that at all, no matter whose thought it was. "I'm bone-stubborn. I'll mule my way through, no matter how hard it is."

But when she did that, she stopped thinking. She went blind to easier ways. She let herself think that everything was impossible, and nothing was simple.

"This isn't simple at all!"

Maybe. Maybe not.

This, thought Rowan, must have been how the old Greeks felt when they went to their oracles. Deeply frustrated, sorely baffled, and not a little angry. She would have done better to find Kerrec and his scrying-pool, for all the good she got out of her mother's advice. If it really was her mother, and not her own rattling brain.

And yet something did come to her as she stalked out of the chapel. It was not much. It was only a straw to grasp at, like the one that had proved to be so useless.

She could do nothing about it now. It was deep night, too early even for monks to be up and at their prayers. She had said all of hers that she could find to say. She went to bed for a while, not to sleep, not much, but she dozed a little. Someday soon she was going to have to remember how to sleep properly.

Father Angilbert was not Rowan's confessor. That was harmless little Father Liutpold with his fluttery blessings and his easy penances. Father Liutpold would hear about all this later—much later, if Rowan was fortunate—but by then it would all be done and only heaven's price to pay.

On this painfully bright morning after her too-wakeful night, she needed someone stronger and less easily frightened than her gentle confessor. Father Angilbert was a dear and much-loved friend, but Rowan would never call him gentle. He had not even been a priest for very long. He had been a poet first, and student and teacher in the school, and would have been Bertha's husband if the Emperor had allowed his daughter to marry. Instead the Emperor had made him an abbot and given him an abbey a good distance from Aachen. But that did not keep Father Angilbert away from Bertha, or from their children, for any longer than it had to. He was in the palace much more often than he was in his abbey; and he was in the palace this morning. He was alone where Rowan had expected to find him, perched on a stool in the scriptorium, copying a book. She peered over his shoulder.

"Lucretius," he said without glancing at her or pausing in the swift procession of his lines, "on the nature of the universe."

"Does he say anything about demons?" Rowan asked.

Angilbert finished the line and began another. "He says that nothing exists but atoms and the void. And maybe gods, but they don't care for human troubles."

"That's dreadfully pagan."

He smiled up at her. He was a handsome man, as fair as Bertha and even taller. He was tonsured as a priest had to be, but on him it looked only faintly ridiculous. "Even demons notice what humans do," he said. "No, I haven't found any demons in Lucretius. Have you been finding them in Aachen?"

"Yes," said Rowan.

He had not been expecting that: his blue eyes widened. Then he laughed, maybe only because she had startled him. "I don't think it's a demon that holds your father captive, little Rowan-tree, unless it's the devil's work for a man to grow old."

Rowan shook her head so hard that she made herself dizzy. "It *is* a demon. It's a spell. I saw it cast on him."

"And you didn't stop it?"

"I tried," she said. "I wasn't strong enough."

"Little Rowan," said Father Angilbert, leaving his book and his pen to take her hands in his, "I'd play your game, but not today. I can't make light of what's fallen on us all."

Rowan pulled free. "Don't talk to me as if I were a weanling child! I tell you it's true. He has a spell on him. I *saw*."

129

He did not believe her. "Rowan, if you saw any-thing, it was a nightmare of your own. The Emperor is ill. That's all, and quite enough."

"But I saw," said Rowan, trying not to whine. "Won't you try to believe me? What harm would it do to chant the exorcism? Sickness is devilry, too. Isn't it?"

"Not that kind," Angilbert said. "I'm not empowered to cast out evil spirits. And even if I were, I know it would do no good with the Emperor. He suffers from a very earthly malady."

"How do you know?"

"I know," said Angilbert.

He was deluded. Enspelled? Rowan could sense no trace of it on him. Maybe there was no need of it. He disbelieved entirely of his own will, and blinded himself to anything that threatened that disbelief.

All the priests were like that. To them she was a child, and a girl besides. Her wits were weak with fear for her father. Of course she would hope for something as easy as a demon. Demons could be cast out. Old age had no cure but death.

All of that, she read in Father Angilbert's clear blue eyes. He was being kind not to rebuke her for inflaming herself with fancies.

"Can you pray for him?" she demanded. "Can you at least do that?"

"Every moment I can," said Father Angilbert.

"Have you come to laugh at me, too?"

Abbess Gisela seemed somewhat taken aback by Rowan's outburst. Rowan, brooding in the stifling closet of her bedchamber, turned her back on her aunt and waited for her to go away.

The abbess did no such thing. Rowan felt her weight on the bed. She did not say anything. Nor would Rowan.

Rowan could not keep a good sulk going with the abbess for audience. Nor could she think, which was what she had come in here to do. Her mind kept running in circles.

"Has it occurred to you," the abbess inquired, "that it's lucky no one believes you? You're confessing openly to witchcraft, after all."

"Does it matter, if it keeps my father alive?"

"Is that really why you do it? Or are you trying to trick everyone into proving that you're lying?"

Rowan whipped about. "I'm not lying!"

"But you wish you were."

"I wish my father were free of the thing that holds him."

"So do we all," said Abbess Gisela.

"But no one will help," said Rowan. "No one will listen."

"Is the master cook no one, then?"

"It didn't do any good."

"So," said the abbess. "If he refuses you, he's not helping. If he fails, he's not helping, either. What will satisfy you? Are you determined that you alone will save your father?"

"I don't care who saves him. I just want him to be saved."

"Commendable," the abbess said. "Your nose is running."

Rowan wiped it angrily on her sleeve. "I'm not crying!"

"Did I say you were?"

The abbess, Rowan realized, was just like her mother. But she could shut her mother out. She could hear Abbess Gisela even through her fingers in her ears.

"What did you try this time?" the abbess asked. "Herbs alone won't help. Nor will prayers, if those were what you were hoping for."

"I was hoping for an exorcism," snapped Rowan.

"I'm not sure that will be of any use either. He's not possessed, or not exactly."

Rowan gaped at her. "You know what's wrong with him? Then how do we cure him?"

"I don't know," the abbess said. She sounded tired of a sudden. "I said we'd find a way, do you remember?" Rowan did, vividly. "I've been looking for one. Every door I try is locked, and every inspiration dies before it's born. Maybe that's a spell, too; a spell of indifference. Do you find yourself not wanting to care, just to let it end as it will?"

"*No,*" said Rowan fiercely.

The abbess sighed. "Of course you don't. Your stubbornness guards you, I think."

That was little enough comfort. Rowan glared. "Are you telling me everybody's spelled? Even you?"

"It's possible," said the abbess. "We're all a part of the empire, and therefore of the Emperor."

"But I'm his own blood."

"And your mother's, too. She had a will like iron. More even than your father has, and he's immovable when he digs his feet in."

Rowan heard that, but her mind had jumped across it to what mattered. "I'll keep trying. Somehow, before it's too late, I'll find a way out of this. If anyone can help me—if anyone will—"

"Don't fancy yourself his only champion," her aunt said dryly. "But by all means do what you can."

"Even if I have to use magic?"

There. She had said it. Abbess Gisela did not even blink. "I'm sure you'll be absolved if you succeed."

"And if I fail, why then, I was never exactly pure of soul."

"No?" The abbess pushed herself to her feet. "You're putting too much trust in men, Theoderada."

"Even priests?"

"Priests above all," the abbess said.

Such grand heresy left no room for astonishment. "But—" said Rowan.

"Trust yourself," said the abbess. "Trust what's in you. Your mother never did. That, more than anything else, was what killed her."

"She died of a fever," Rowan said.

"So they'll say of your father, maybe. Or that he's dying of an apoplexy."

"Then who—what—my mother—"

"Does it matter? She's dead. Your father will be soon, unless someone finds a way to win back his soul for him."

"If you have so much knowledge," Rowan said harshly, "why aren't you doing it yourself?"

"Because I have knowledge," said the abbess, "but no magic."

Rowan felt as if she had caught a fever: hot, then

cold; heart beating; thoughts fluttering like birds in a hawk's shadow. "Then teach me," she said. "Teach me everything I need to know."

"I can't," said the abbess.

Rowan stopped short. "You—"

"I can't," the abbess repeated. "I've told you all I know. I can't teach you magic, and magic, I very much fear, is what you need."

"There must be someone else," said Rowan. "There has to be magic greater than I have, or than—*he*—has." She did not mean Michael Phokias; she meant Kerrec. Her aunt might not understand. She said it, to make it clear. "The Breton. He's a witch's son, of a line of witches."

"One is greater than either of you," said the abbess.

And she meant Michael Phokias. Rowan's stomach hurt as it always did when she thought of him. "You're telling me it's useless, no matter what we do."

"No," said the abbess.

"And you're telling me," Rowan blundered on, "that I should leave the path of righteousness, and damn myself for my father's sake."

"I don't think magic is damnation," the abbess said. "Nor would you, if you had a grain of sense. Who's had the teaching of you? I'd like to box his ears."

"Father Alcuin, before he went back to York—Father Angilbert—"

"Learned and line-spouting fools," said Abbess Gisela. "Your elephant-boy is worth a dozen of them."

"Kerrec is the most ill-spoken, arrogant, exasperating—"

"He reminds you of yourself," her aunt said sweetly. "He has a key to this, I think. So do you. Only neither of you knows what it is, or how to use it."

Rowan was tired of arguing, tired of fighting, tired of thinking. All she wanted to do was lie down and forget. But she was not being allowed to do that. "Will we have time to learn?" she asked her aunt, less sharply than she might have, and more wearily.

"I pray so," said Abbess Gisela.

Thirteen

. . . .

*A*ND THERE they were again, Rowan and Kerrec and the Elephant, no better off than they had been before, and who knew how much worse.

"I tried," Rowan said. "I tried to find someone else to help."

"There isn't anyone else," said Kerrec. He had wheedled the Elephant out of his stall, and was trying to get him to give himself a bath in the swans' pond. Rowan would have liked to see him do as he loved to do, draw the water into his trunk and spray it over his back, and if he was feeling particularly playful he sprayed everyone else, too, till they were all gloriously wet.

The sunlight was not kind to him now. It showed how thin he was, and how pale and dry his skin had grown. Parts of it were almost white, and it was shedding in patches. She would not have been surprised if he had lain down and not got up again, as feeble as he looked.

"I think we have to force a battle," Rowan said.

Kerrec stared at her from the middle of the pool. He had managed to get the Elephant in, but Abul Abbas only stood there with the water lapping his feet and the end of his trunk, and the swans hissing at him from the safety of the pool's far edge. "We tried that before," said Kerrec. "Or have you forgotten already? It didn't help us at all."

"Then I think we were missing something we should have had." Rowan was letting the words come out of the place where the magic was. It was not easy or particularly comfortable, but it felt necessary. Much of magic, she was beginning to think, was in letting it work itself, and staying out of its way.

"What are we missing?" Kerrec asked. "Besides strength?"

"That's just it," said Rowan. "We didn't have any strength. All we had was desperation."

"But we don't have anything but ourselves. We can't be stronger than we are."

"Even both of us together, the way we were the first time we did magic?" Rowan shivered in spite of herself. "And suppose we got help."

"Who will help us? You just finished telling me that no one would."

"That's because I was asking people to do it *for* us. I'm going to ask them to do it *with* us."

Kerrec's expression was angry, but Rowan thought he was more wary than anything else. "Ask people here? To work magic?"

"Father Angilbert won't help," said Rowan, "but I think Bertha will. Bertha's sensible. And so is Aunt Gisela. She showed me the way, after a fashion. She said I was looking to the men."

He flushed at that. "Then what am I?"

"You're a Breton witch," Rowan answered him. "And that makes you a bit more than a man."

He was not mollified, not even a little. "I don't do women's magic."

"Is there such a thing? Or is it all one, and people choose which parts they'll do?" There. That stopped him short. Rowan did not take time to feel triumphant. "And," she said, "there's something else we all forgot. Or someone else."

Was the Elephant reviving a tiny fraction? Had his dulled eye turned to her?

She tucked up her skirt and waded into the pool, and touched his shoulder where the grey had faded to the color of chalk. It was warm. She wondered if elephants got fevers as humans did, or if it was simply the sun on his hide. "My Lord Abul Abbas," she said, "can you help us?"

Of course he might not understand her. He only ever talked to Kerrec, and who knew what languages of men he understood, if he understood any at all? But she had to try. She would try anything, if it would break the Byzantine's spell.

The Elephant sighed hugely. He was not going to listen, or else he did not know to. "Kerrec," she started to say, to ask him to see if he could make the Elephant understand.

Then Abul Abbas stirred. His trunk came up. It wobbled, as if he had half forgotten how to use it, but in a moment it steadied. It wrapped itself very gently about her shoulders and tugged. She let it lead her to where he wanted her, in front of him. It slipped from her shoulders, snaked down to the water. She heard the suck and gurgle as he sucked up a trunkful.

If he was going to drench her, she was going to be very annoyed. His trunk arched out of the water, over his back, and sprayed a mighty stream. He seemed almost to be laughing.

"He's happy," Kerrec said in wonder. "He's dancing inside of himself."

She could feel it. It made her laugh, if with a catch in it. "He was trying to tell us, but even you wouldn't listen, or you didn't know how."

Kerrec resented that, she could see, but the Elephant's gladness took the edge off. "He did tell me . . . something. I couldn't hear him clearly. I thought he wanted us to get the Talisman back."

"So he did," said Rowan, thinking hard as she spoke, "but he meant us to be three instead of two. And we went and tried to do it ourselves, without him, and the spell caught him, and he couldn't say anything till we said it first."

The Elephant seemed to nod, eagerly, Rowan thought.

Kerrec was listening intently to what must be a flood of Elephant-words. "The spell binds speech. It did that with your father. It binds everything that would let a man or an animal do anything for himself. After a while he dies, because he can't eat, or even will to live."

"But all we had to do was know it, and say it to him," said Rowan. "Maybe, if we go to my father—"

"No," said Kerrec, and he looked as downcast as she felt. "Abul Abbas says that's not so. He knew what was happening and was able to guard himself, and to hope that we'd see the obvious before it was too late." That must have been exactly what the Elephant said, and not too kindly either: there were spots of color on Kerrec's cheeks. "He says that you have very good eyes when you bother to use them. And you know much more than you think you know."

"What does that mean?" Rowan asked.

"He says you should know."

She glowered at the Elephant. He was giving himself a thorough and soaking bath. The swans had fled the pool altogether. She was getting wet, but it felt wonderful, even if she was out of temper again. "You're just as bad as everyone else. *What* should I know?"

"You know," said Kerrec.

Rowan would have slapped him if he had been in reach. A kicking, scratching, shrieking fight would have felt as good to her as the Elephant's bath did to him.

Sometimes she was sorry that she had learned to be civilized. Words were a poor second to a real and gratifying free-for-all.

She sloshed out of the pool and sat on the grass, which was as damp as she was. Kerrec stayed with the Elephant. She watched them play at splash-and-spray, and thought that the Elephant was still more white than grey, but he did not look quite as sickly as he had before. Were there white elephants, like white stags? And were they holy, or at least magical, as white stags were?

She thought maybe they were. Maybe that was one

of the things Abul Abbas said she knew without knowing it. As she had known that they needed him to make the magic stronger, and had been supremely foolish not to think of him the first time they faced Michael Phokias. That was their fault, for thinking that he was only an animal, for all his wisdom. Kerrec at least should have known better.

She crushed that thought before it had time to grow. This was not the time to lay blame. She had to discover what else she knew, that the Elephant had seen and would not tell her.

That meant looking her magic in the face. She thought she had been doing it in admitting that it existed, and using it when she had to. But she had only been edging round it, and evading it, and trying not to think about it. She was like a girl given a knife and told that she had to use it, picking it up gingerly in two fingers, and dropping it as soon as she thought she safely could.

This time Rowan knew she had to grasp her magic by the hilt and hold it as it was meant to be held. She even saw it as a knife, sitting on the grass in front of her. It was a long knife, a short sword, one of the vicious-looking thick-bladed things that came down from the old Romans. It looked like what it was: a tool for killing men.

"No," she said to herself, not caring if Kerrec heard. "That's not the image I need." Her magic was not made for killing. It wanted to break a spell, and to heal the harm the spell had wrought.

"Not a knife, then," she said, "or a sword. A Talisman—yes. Yes!" She could see it clear in front of her.

Its chain was the spell that bound her father. The Talisman itself was the magic, bright gold and terrible, but still a part of her. Where the relic was in the real Talisman, the one that the sorcerer had ruined, was a glowing coal. That was the heart of her magic.

"All I have to do," she said to herself, to the air, to the Elephant and his boy, "is take it up and put it on." It was the hardest thing she had ever contemplated.

Kerrec was standing next to her. He could not do it for her, or help much at all. Oddly, because so much that he did irritated her so profoundly, she was glad of his presence.

There was something in that, that she should think about.

Now she had to focus herself on this one, necessary task. She must take up the whole of her magic.

She stretched out her hand. It was her real and fleshly hand, but it was something else as well, something more. It paused over the golden talisman that was so like her father's Talisman, lying on the grass beside the swans' pool. The fire in the jewel was burning hot; it seared her palm. She flinched.

No. She must not draw back. She must reach, so, and touch the talisman. She gasped. It hurt, oh heaven it hurt.

"No, it doesn't." Kerrec, soft lest he startle her, but very firm. "That's your resistance, lying to you to make you run away. Make it stop."

"How do I stop pain?" she demanded, breathless with it.

"Lean your will against it."

How astonishing: he was actually telling her what she needed to know. The touch of irony cooled the fire a little. She tried leaning as Kerrec said. "It doesn't do a bit of—" Her teeth clicked together.

It was like snuffing out a lamp. One moment, red fire. The next, nothing. The talisman felt cool and solid, though she knew it was not real. Its chain was dreadfully heavy. She strained to lift it. How was she to bear that weight around her neck?

The same way, her common sense told her, that she had borne the fire: by willing it to go away. This was not as fast, and not as easy. It came by painful inches, straining at her fingers, seeming to grow heavier, the higher she raised it. Then all at once, between one breath and the next, the terrible weight was gone. The shape of her magic was light in her hand, swinging on its chain just level with her heart. She felt as if she had moved a mountain.

"Don't stop," Kerrec said in her ear. "Don't think. Put it on."

Habit would have made her argue. Sense made her obey. The golden thing settled on her breast as if it had always been there—and in truth it had been, only she had not known it.

Her hands fell away from the talisman. She closed her eyes and simply thought about breathing.

When she opened them, the world had changed.

It was the same world she had always known, green of grass and trees, brown of earth, blue of sky. And yet the green was brighter, the brown deeper, the blue clearer than she had ever imagined they could be. She gasped with the wonder of them; and gasped again as her eyes turned to the Elephant. He was pure white, shining like snow on Candlemas Day. And Kerrec—ragged dusty-haired Kerrec—was full of light.

"There now," he said. "You're the magic's master. Don't let it rule you."

"But—" she started to say. Then forgot, because she had looked down, and she was like a lamp at dusk. For a moment she did not realize what she had not seen. She could feel the talisman, its chain about her neck, its weight on her breast, but there was nothing to see with eyes of body or mind. It had become a part of her.

Her eyes closed again. She did not know if she could stand to see like this, not every waking moment. She *leaned*, and carefully, slowly, opened her eyes.

Everything was dull; blessedly, beautifully so. This was the world she remembered. The Elephant was grey blotched with sickly white, Kerrec was his untidy self, she was Rowan in a muddy gown, sitting by the swans' pond in her father's palace in Aachen.

But inside she was all different.

"I still don't know what I know," she said.

"You'll know it when you need it," Kerrec told her. "You're lucky. You've got the gift of knowing. I had to learn everything step by step, with mistakes that could have killed me."

"That won't happen to me?"

"You're still as human as you always were. You can still make mistakes. But you don't need to learn how."

"I don't have to learn to make mistakes? I can't tell

you how that comforts me." She shrugged him off before he could answer. The sun dazzled her, shining straight in her eyes. She started. "How did it get so late? It was barely noon when I came here."

"Magic's time is tricky," Kerrec said.

Rowan tensed. "But if it takes so long to get through a few moments, what will happen when we meet the sorcerer? He'll be gone and my father will be dead before I can get my wits together."

"I said it was tricky," said Kerrec. "Not that it was slow. Or not always. It takes as long as it needs to take. You may find it moving very fast, when we come to the battle."

"And it is going to be a battle," Rowan said. She was starting to shake. "I've never fought. Men fight. Women stay home and wait, and tend the wounded."

"This isn't that kind of fighting," Kerrec said. "You said yourself that magic isn't male or female, it just is. So is war of magic. Or are you going to run away again, and leave everything to fend for itself?"

He was trying to shock her into courage. She would not have known that, an hour or two ago. It made her no less angry now, but she was quicker to recover. "You know there's no escape for me. Not since I took up my magic. The sorcerer will know, if he doesn't already. And if I don't go to face him, he'll come after me. He can't let me live and wield magic this close to his sorceries."

"He can if he's diverted."

"By you?"

Kerrec did not answer.

"He'll gut you and hang you up to dry," Rowan said.

"Not if I'm with Abul Abbas."

Abul Abbas rumbled. Maybe it was his stomach demanding its dinner. Maybe he was saying something of Kerrec's foolishness.

"It has to be all three," Rowan said. "Threes have power, you told me. Now I understand what you meant. We three are different sides of magic. You have sight. I have knowing. Abul Abbas has—" She paused as the rest of it came to her. "Abul Abbas has wisdom and strength. And he knows the Talisman. He's part of it somehow."

"They used the magic in him to seal it, when it was made," Kerrec said slowly, listening to the Elephant, turning thoughts into words where Rowan could hear. "The two of them are the same gift. The Talisman was to protect your father. Abul Abbas was to protect the Talisman. And he failed. We got in his way when he would have stopped the spell; it rebounded on him. We were idiots!"

"We didn't know," said Rowan.

"It's going to be hard," Kerrec said. "Much harder than it would have been at first."

"Then the sooner we do it," said Rowan, "the sooner it's done."

He should have known better than to be surprised. "Now?"

"What better time will there be?"

That called for an hour's worth of answers, or none. Kerrec opened his mouth, but shut it again. Rowan nodded briskly. "Good," she said. "Now. Shall we begin?"

Fourteen

. . . .

*B*EGINNING WAS EASY enough to say, but harder to do. Before they could engage in battle, they had to find the enemy. And Michael Phokias was nowhere to be found.

The envoys from Byzantium had rooms in the palace. Some of them were there, asleep. Others were in the town doing whatever men did in the early evening; most of it had to do with wine and women, and some with song. None of them was Michael Phokias.

Rowan knew a long moment's horror. What if he had gone away? What if he had taken the blackened and corrupted Talisman and gone back to his master in Byzantium, and left his spell to work itself unattended?

But that did not feel like Michael Phokias. He would want to see the end of it, and his master, if he was sensible, would want clear proof that the spell had succeeded. No, Michael Phokias had not left Aachen. He was hidden, that was all, and she had to find him.

First Rowan did something that she should have thought to do long since. She sought her eldest sister, and found her in the company of their aunt. That, taken all in all, was not surprising. And it made matters simpler.

"Bertha," said Rowan as soon as she politely could, "would you watch over Gisela for me?"

Rowan had tried not to let that come out of nowhere, but to Bertha no doubt it did, since they had been discussing the chance of rain before morning. Bertha looked mildly startled, but she was calm by nature, and she was used to Rowan's shifts and changes. "Why?" she asked. "What do you think she'll do? Shouldn't it be Hrotrud I watch?"

"Hrotrud doesn't need watching," Rowan said, trying not to snap. "She hasn't been acting like a mooncalf in a stupor."

"Gisela is never the most vivacious of women," said Bertha. But her brows had drawn together. "And yet . . . she is acting strangely, isn't she? Do you think she's ill, Theoderada?"

"I think she's bewitched," Rowan said, and never mind what Bertha thought.

The abbess nodded, agreeing, but not saying anything aloud.

Bertha's frown deepened, maybe at that evidence of the abbess' complicity, maybe only at what Rowan had said. "Rowan, do you think you're seeing things quite as they are?"

"I don't know," said Rowan with as much patience as she could muster. "All I know is that she needs a guard. Can't you do that, Bertha? I don't know of anybody who would be better at it."

Abbess Gisela spoke at last before Bertha could begin, neatly forestalling her. "We'll keep the vigil," she said.

Bertha opened her mouth, probably to object, but closed it again and sighed. She was not won over, not nearly, but she would do as the abbess bade her.

Rowan hugged them both hard enough to squeeze the breath from them, and left before she could be tempted to linger till morning.

With Gisela as well protected as she could be, Rowan went in search of Kerrec. That was easier than she might have expected. When she thought of him, she knew exactly where to go.

More magic. More oddness. And yet it was like coming home, to find him near the outer gate of the menagerie. His rough-haired shadow was blessedly familiar in a world that kept trying to go strange, his voice as close to friendly as it ever was, calling her by name. "Kerrec," she answered him.

"Names have power," he said. "That's another lesson for you." Then he lowered his voice. "I think I've found him."

Everything in Rowan sprang alert. She found herself whispering, as if the sorcerer could not have heard them from a mile off, naming themselves without concealment. "Where is he? And where is Abul Abbas?"

Kerrec answered the second question first. "He's waiting. He'll be with us when we need him."

"But—" said Rowan.

"We have to start alone; make the enemy think there's no more to us than there was before. When Abul Abbas is ready, he'll come."

Rowan shook her head. That was wrong, she knew it. How could the Elephant not know it, too?

But Kerrec had her by the arm, dragging her till she had to walk of her own accord or fall flat. Time was short, too short for arguments. And if they failed because they were two instead of three—

She had to trust Abul Abbas.

Once she was walking, Kerrec let her go. He was trusting her, maybe because he had no choice. As softly as she could, and with something of the resignation of the condemned criminal approaching the headsman's block, Rowan followed where he led.

Someone had oiled the hinges of the gate to the menagerie. That was new: it had creaked in ghastly fashion when Rowan last went through it. It served them well now, letting them enter without a sound.

The menagerie was transformed in the pallid light of the moon. Its shadows were utter black, its bright places luminous blue-white. Shapes could be anything: cages with beasts asleep inside, swans in the pool, peacocks together under the beech tree.

Not every creature slept. Rowan heard the soft growling of the leopard and the pad-pad-pad of its pacing. Others of the big cats were uneasy, and the apes chittered as they dreamed. Eyes gleamed in the depths of the bear's cage. Beyond it in the hunting park she heard the sound of bodies moving, and the chuff of a stag startled into vigilance.

She caught at Kerrec's hand. It was cold, but no colder than her own. The touch warmed them both a little. Linked hand to hand like children frightened of the dark, they crept toward the center of the uneasiness.

She could feel it on her skin like the touch of an icy wind, and like wind it tugged at her, striving to thrust her back. Because of the force of the unease, they had to take a winding path, round the swans' pool and back to the wall. That was not a way Rowan often took, since it was so roundabout, but on the other side of the wall was the orchard where so much of this tangle had begun.

The moon shone through the apple boughs, dappling the grass. It was a waning moon, and sickly, white and bloated like a corpse. The trees seemed as twisted as the moon; the apples on them swelled not with ripeness but with rot.

Rowan stopped and could not go on. Kerrec, who should have pulled her back into motion, was as frozen-stark as she. There was nothing to see but moon and trees and leprous grass.

She set her teeth and shook the horrible vision out of her head. Here was the orchard as it had always been, and the moon, and the night untainted by any foulness. "There's no one here," she started to say; thinking that this was a trick, and the sorcerer was somewhere far away.

Kerrec's hand tightened on hers till she gasped with the pain. Whether it was her pain or his tautness, all at once she could see. Someone knelt under the centermost tree, doing something in the grass.

He was cutting a circle with a knife that cast no light from its blade, even when it should have caught the moon and flashed. He was careful about it, meticulous, but very quick.

Something lay in the circle. It seemed a bundle of clothing, or maybe a carpet, until Rowan understood the oddities of its shape. It was a human body. Its hair was long and pale. It was a woman, then; old, maybe, with that white hair.

Not if white was silvery gold, and the woman was Gisela.

Rowan was letting her fears conquer her common sense. Gisela was asleep in her chamber, guarded by the strongest women Rowan knew.

But Gisela was here, covered with a cloak. She stirred slightly and murmured as one does in sleep.

She was alive, then, and probably enspelled.

The figure who made the circle straightened just before he closed it, and turned his face to the moon. Yes, it was Michael Phokias, with his curling black beard and his long pale face. His eyes were black and lightless like the blade of his dagger.

"Black magic," Kerrec breathed. "Oh, black indeed."

Rowan kicked him to make him hush. The sorcerer did not know that they were there—he was too arrogant to set wards, or too contemptuous of their magic—and they did not need to awaken him to his mistake. It might be all the advantage they had, without Abul Abbas.

She wondered if young warriors felt this way before a fight, half dizzy, half sick, and thoroughly terrified. So terrified that she could not move, either forward or back.

At last she shook herself. She would not die here, if she could possibly help it. Nor would she go away ensorceled.

That too, maybe, was a warrior's thought, his last desperate surge of courage before the charge.

The sorcerer bent over the woman asleep in his unfinished circle, and lifted her cloak. Under it she was as white as the moon, and as bare as she was born. He did not pause to savor the sight of her, though he took her hands and folded them on her breast. Something dark was wound in her fingers, something darker than that hidden beneath them.

Rowan's hand went to her own breast, where her magic pulsed like a heart.

Gisela had the Talisman again. But Gisela belonged to the sorcerer, in body if not in soul. And he was stepping away from her, out of his circle, and bending, and sinking his knife in the earth, and closing the wall that was made of magic, with Gisela inside.

Rowan had seen enough and more than enough. And so, it seemed, had Kerrec. Even before she moved, he was ahead of her, running, crying something in Breton.

"Bloody *idiot*," she said. It no longer mattered whether the sorcerer could hear her. He must know that where Kerrec was, there was Rowan.

She ran forward a step or two, but she was not as fast as Kerrec, especially in skirts; and one rash fool was enough for any army. She could feel as well as hear him, calling in his magic as he ran, but he could hardly summon it all before he blundered into the sorcerer's circle.

Easily, almost contemptuously, the sorcerer drew back the hand that held the knife, and let it fly.

Rowan gasped and cursed herself for not running after all. But though Kerrec might be an idiot, he was a keen-eyed idiot. He ducked, slid, stumbled on a hummock in the grass, went down to one knee. The knife passed harmlessly overhead and buried itself in earth. Rowan could hear it hissing like a snake cheated of its prey.

Kerrec spoke, this time in Frankish. "You must be weak, Greekling, to forget your subtlety."

"With you I need none," said Michael Phokias. He raised his hand again, flung again. Rowan had seen him reach for no weapon, but one was there, black like the knife he had flung before, narrow and wickedly pointed, aiming straight for Kerrec's heart.

Kerrec was not so lucky this time. He threw himself flat. The dart of magic followed him down. His hand flew up. The dart glanced off it and fell as the knife had, biting deep in the grass.

His gasp was distinct. There was no darkness of blood on his palm, but there was pain—it was written in his face.

"Twice you have escaped me," Michael Phokias said. "Who would have thought it?" With no more warning than that, he grasped a shaft of moonlight that slanted through the boughs, and hefted it like a spear.

Kerrec, helpless on the ground, could do no more than scramble backward, away from the terrible, impos-

154

sible weapon. The sorcerer did not even grant him the honor of laughter, only shortened the spear and stabbed, as a man does with a wounded beast.

As the dart flew, Rowan's feet untangled at last. She stretched into a run. When the spear thrust down, she caught hold of it—gasping, for it was cold, colder than ice—and bent the whole of her weight and her speed into hurling it aside.

It was almost not enough. The cold of the spear was so terrible, the sorcerer's strength so great, that she seemed a shape of air against them.

But Michael Phokias was taken thoroughly by surprise. So, almost, was Rowan. She had been sure that he knew she was there.

Startlement and the shock of being thwarted where he had thought himself invincible came together to slow his hand when he should have turned the spear on her. But she still had hold of it; her hands were locked on it, frozen. She wrenched the thing out of his grip.

As soon as he let go, the spear melted into moonlight. Rowan, braced for weight and for agony, stumbled back and nearly fell. Her hands clenched shut in a spasm, then sprang open. She stared at them wildly, looking for the fingers to stiffen and drop off, or for the palms to be blackened and blistered with cold. But they bore no mark, not even a hint of the pain that had tormented them.

That pause might have been her downfall, if Michael Phokias had mustered wits and magic in time. By God's good grace, he seemed as fuddled as she.

Kerrec was up in a crouch, gathered to spring. Rowan blocked his path. "What are you doing with my sister?" she demanded of the sorcerer.

He should have known to expect something of the sort, instead of gaping at her like a man caught napping in the middle of a battle.

Maybe that was a trap. Byzantines were subtle. Michael Phokias might be trying to make her scorn him, so that she would weaken, and be ripe for the kill.

He looked thoroughly nonplussed. Still he answered boldly, with no fear of her at all. "Your sister is . . . assisting me in a matter of magic."

"Does she know she's doing it?"

Kerrec was hissing. He would be thinking that Rowan was infinitely stupid, giving the sorcerer time to work new sorceries while he bandied words with her. But Rowan knew that the sorcerer could not talk and chant spells at the same time. Michael Phokias' magic was word-magic. Not like Kerrec's, that was of the eye and the mind, or Rowan's, that was of the heart.

So she kept him talking, until she could think of a way to disarm him. His eyes were fixed on her. She wished there were a way to tell Kerrec to break the circle, step into it, take the Talisman from Gisela. Frantic waving behind her back was no use at all.

The sorcerer was saying something. Rowan made herself listen. "Your sister knows that I have need of her. She gave herself without demur."

"Because you laid a spell on her," Rowan said. "You can't use the Talisman without her, can you? Not as well as you want to. Otherwise my father would be dead."

"Your father is old. He was struck ill on the hunt."

Rowan wanted to spit. "Don't tell lies, sorcerer. I was there. I know what you did. Took you all night and most of the day, didn't it? And laid you out flat for days."

If she alarmed him with the accuracy of her guess, he did not show it. "You are a perceptive child. You are also a meddlesome one. What if I told you that I need your sister's blood to complete the working?"

Rowan's ears buzzed. She had not heard that. No. She had not.

Idiot. Of course she had. "You're trying to scare me."

"Why should I trouble myself? Yes, the first working was insufficient, and taxed me far more than I expected. I had thought—hoped—to perform my task without resort to extreme measures."

"Such as cutting out my sister's heart?"

"No, no," said the sorcerer, and he honestly seemed appalled. "That is barbaric. I would open the veins of her arms, and give her blood to the earth, and grant her the easiest death of all, a death of slow and deepening sleep."

"Still," said Rowan, "death is death. And blood is blood. Does it have to be Gisela?"

"She is of your father's blood."

Rowan nodded slowly. Kerrec, she noticed, had not moved. She could just see him out of the corner of her eye, white shocked face, absolute stillness. Why in the world could he not see what she was trying to do, and help her?

Then he shifted infinitesimally. Rowan almost exclaimed aloud. He was closer to the circle than he had been. He had been moving, but by degrees, as a hunter does when he stalks his prey.

She wished that he would find a way to go faster. Though she had the sorcerer's attention now, who knew how long that would last?

Her mind wrenched back to what the sorcerer had said. Gisela's blood. Her father's blood. The Talisman, meant for the Emperor, accepting the touch of his daughter, but serving a stranger only by force.

"Does it have to be Gisela?" Rowan asked again. "Only Gisela? Not any other child of the Emperor?"

Behind her, Kerrec gasped. He was almost beside the circle. The sorcerer said, "Give it up, witch-lad. Even should you pierce the circle, you can never touch the Talisman."

"But I can," said Rowan. "Can't I?"

"You can," said Michael Phokias. It was hard to see in the moonlight, but his eyes seemed to gleam on her. "Are you offering yourself?"

"Would it set Gisela free?"

"Rowan," said Kerrec. "Rowan, for God's sake—"

"So that is what they call you," the sorcerer said. "Rowan. The tree that guards against magic. Do they know how appropriate that is?"

So, thought Rowan, shivering. He knew about names, too, and the magic that was in names. She pressed the little advantage it gave her. "Would it set Gisela free if I offered myself in her place?"

"Why do you offer? You think little enough of her, from all that I can see."

"She's family," Rowan said. "Would it?"

"You are obstinate," said Michael Phokias, not without approval. "Yes, it would. Splendidly. She has no magic whatsoever. You have enough to make matters interesting. And yet," he said as if the thought had just occurred to him, which Rowan very much doubted, "if you give your blood to the spell, your father dies. Is your beautiful brainless sister worth the life of the Emperor of the West?"

"Gisela isn't brainless," said Rowan, "and you don't believe for a minute that Father deserves that title." And not for a moment did she intend to give her blood to the spell. She would fight with everything she had, and hope that once she had the Talisman in her hand—as surely she must, or the spell would not be complete—it would help her to turn the sorcery against the sorcerer.

It was desperate, and it hardly counted as a plan, but it was the best she could think of.

Michael Phokias was staring at her. If he could read what she was thinking, then she was lost, and everything else, too. "You believe," he said, "that you have some hope."

"What do you want?" she asked him sharply. "What do you gain from this?"

"The so-called Emperor of the West dies," he answered, "and the one and true and only Emperor of the Romans rules unchallenged."

"My father really is a threat to Byzantium, then. You wouldn't bother with him if he weren't."

"Say rather that we prefer to live untormented by gnats who call themselves emperors."

Rowan refused to be stung by the insult. "Set my sister free, and I'll give myself into your hands." She held out her own, offering what she had to give. Magic, too. She tried to think it into a shape that would tempt him; not easy when she had no idea what that might be.

Kerrec growled. He sounded so much like one of the Emperor's boarhounds that Rowan nearly forgot herself and laughed. But all urge to laughter died as he sprang past her, toward the circle.

His body jerked as he touched it, and visibly slowed; his face contorted with effort or with pain. But he thrust himself through. He fell to hands and knees beside Gisela, who slept on, with the Talisman on her breast.

Once more Michael Phokias was taken by surprise. Kerrec's leap had broken the circle. The magic dissipated even as they all paused: Rowan sensed it as a fading stink, something like a long-dead fish, and something like a bog in summer.

Kerrec scrambled away from Gisela. Rowan drew breath to shout at him. But she held her tongue when she saw what he was doing. He should not have been able to efface the knife's deep track in the earth, yet as his hands pressed over the place where the circle had been, the earth healed, the grass closed where it had been cut apart.

Rowan scraped together her wits. "Kerrec," she said, "it's no use. He's still stronger than either of us. Go away while his patience holds, and leave me to the bargain I've made."

The last of the circle vanished under Kerrec's hands. His path had brought him level with Rowan; he looked up into her face. His eyes were enormous, and seemed half blind. She felt something groping toward her like a hand, but his hands were flat on the ground, holding it together. He wanted something, was trying to tell her something.

She could not hear it. The sorcerer was gathering his power; that too she felt, a scorching on her skin, though he seemed to be standing mute and amazed. His lips moved without sound, making his magic of the word and the will.

Sweet saints, she thought, or prayed. *Where is Abul Abbas?*

No answer came. There was only herself to trust, then, and nothing else in the world. She breathed deep and sprang; flung herself at the sorcerer, wrapped arms around him, fastened her lips on his.

It would have worked better if she had had any practice. Hrotrud would have known how. As it was, she just missed getting a mouthful of beard, and her lips ground on his teeth. There was nothing pleasant about it at all.

But it did stop his spellcasting, however briefly. What she had not bargained on was that he would give in to it. She did not even know what he was doing till he did it, it happened so fast. Suddenly his arms were around her, and he was fastened on her like a leech, bending her back till she felt as if she would snap in two.

His breath whuffed in her throat. He was laughing at her. She gagged and fought, but he was too strong.

Stupid, stupid, stupid, stupid, stupid.

It was monotonous, even for a litany, but it was dreadfully, horridly true.

Her magic struggled as fiercely as she did, but it had another focus: not to get away but to get closer. She tried to pull it back, but it was as strong as the Byzantine was. It had turned on her. It had betrayed her.

She sagged in despair. To her astonishment, she found an inch of yielding where none had been before. She worked her fist into it and thrust herself free.

She had no time to gasp, rub her bruised mouth, spit, gag, curse, do anything that would leave her vulnerable. She lunged toward the broken circle and the ruined Talisman.

Michael Phokias caught her arm and wrenched her about. Her shoulder screamed, almost twisting out of its socket. She made no sound. He was chanting, this time aloud, words that made the flesh shudder on her bones.

She flailed, but he held her too far away from him, and too firmly, for a blow to land. His chanting went on. She could not see Kerrec; the sorcerer was in the way.

Then she heard him. Kerrec had a clear voice when he sang, matching word to word of the sorcerer's chant. The chant was a sequence of jarring discords. The song wove with them, shaping them into a rough harmony.

Rowan could sing, but not like this. She tried to pull the sorcerer off balance, to make him lose his place in the chant. No use. No more use than her magic that tried to find chinks in his, and creep into them, and make them gape wide. For every one she found, another one closed in a smooth wall, and his guard grew stronger, the harder she strove to break it.

Kerrec was losing his fight, too. His first flat note was shocking; his second was inevitable. They made the discord worse than it had been before, and strengthened the sorcerer, and therefore the sorcery.

He kept trying, as Rowan did, because there was nothing else they could do, just the two of them, without the third to make them whole. If she could only reach the Talisman, only touch it for a moment, she would win the strength that she lacked, but the Talisman was hopelessly out of reach. Kerrec could not come to it, either, or he would have done so long since.

The sorcerer was laughing as he sang. He was almost done with his working.

Almost, thought Rowan with a spark of hope. He had to let her go if he wanted to shed Gisela's blood. She stopped trying to get away, and got a grip on his arm, holding as tight as he had been holding her.

He saw what she was doing. His arm tensed. Before she could brace against it, he flung her away.

As he flung her out, she flung herself in. She came crashing down on top of Kerrec, inside the broken circle.

The chanting stopped. The sorcerer looked down at the tangle that they made, and smiled. "There," he said, "I have you exactly as I want you."

Fifteen

*R*OWAN UNTANGLED HERSELF from Kerrec. He was breathing, but he seemed as unconscious as Gisela, who had slept through everything and looked ready to sleep till the Last Judgment.

Rowan stretched out a hand. She was not surprised or much frightened to find that it met a wall of air. The wall's bottom bit deep in the earth as the black knife had before Kerrec worked his healing magic. She could touch it without pain, but she could not step past it.

And her magic was on the other side of it.

Not so long ago, she would have danced with joy to find it gone. Now she felt as if she had lost a limb.

Michael Phokias, she had noticed already, was not given to gloating. It was rather disappointing. Evil wizards always gloated. Michael Phokias simply went about his business. Maybe that was Byzantine, to be so practical about everything, even summoning demons.

"How are you going to sacrifice me if I'm in here and you're out there?" she asked him.

An ordinary person would have been in shrieking hysterics. Rowan had been brought up better than that.

Michael Phokias did not remark on her coolness. He had seen enough of it already, Rowan supposed. She was rather sorry. It would have made things easier if he had kept on being startled by her refusal to act like a self-respecting flutterbrain.

"Take the Talisman from your sister," he commanded her.

Rowan blinked. Her mind did not want to work in the direction he was going. "What if I won't?"

"The demon eats you," he said.

"But it will eat me anyway, won't it?"

"Take it," said the sorcerer, and his voice was different. It rang like a great bell. She watched as if from outside as her body turned, stooped, reached.

A palm's width from the Talisman, her hand stopped.

"Resist the warding," the sorcerer said.

He was laying a spell on her. Without thinking, she reached for her magic, to turn his command back on him. But it was still trapped outside the circle, and she was trapped within, apart from it.

"Resist the warding," the sorcerer said again. "Take the Talisman."

She pushed. It was like pressing against a firm cushion, except that cushions did not dissolve fraction by fraction, shrinking to the thinnest of skins about her sister and the Talisman. The Talisman was hot under the shield of its protection, burning with fire-heat.

This was just like the taking of that other talisman

which was her magic, even to the degree and kind of the pain. If she could have protested, she would have done so, loudly. Twice was twice too often.

She clasped the Talisman and bent, raising her sister's head, slipping the chain from about her neck. Gisela's brow wrinkled in a frown. Her head began to toss from side to side.

"Sleep," said the sorcerer. Rowan froze, but the command was not meant for her. Gisela sighed and went slack.

Rowan straightened with the Talisman swinging on its chain. It was all blackened and dull. It should have been nigh invisible in the moonlight, and yet it was so much darker than the darkness that it almost seemed to glow, as if light and not-light could be kin.

A spark woke in the Talisman's center. The crystal opened like an eye, blood-red, slit-pupiled.

Rowan made a sound halfway between a gasp and a shriek, and flung the thing away.

She tried to fling it, at least. The chain coiled about her fingers, flexing like a living thing.

That was enough. Royal upbringing or no, Rowan was not going to stand helpless in a sorcerer's circle with a demon wrapped around her hand, staring at her with its single ghastly eye.

Her free hand got hold of the chain and slowly, struggling not to shake, peeled it off like a glove. Then it wanted to cling to that hand instead, but she was ready for it; just as it started to coil, she shook it off. It dropped writhing to the grass.

Michael Phokias had been shouting for a while. Rowan struggled not to listen. The Talisman's chain was like a snake with a broken back; it whipped and lashed but could not move forward. The weight of the head, the Talisman itself, was too heavy. The eye looked angry: it was redder than it had been, fire-red.

She looked about wildly for something to cover it with. Gisela's cloak lay forgotten on the ground. Snatching it up, Rowan dropped it over the Talisman.

The lashing of the chain-tail stopped. Rowan remembered to breathe.

She had not accomplished anything worth bragging about. She was still trapped in the circle, and Michael Phokias was still outside of it, and now he was angry. His arms swept up in a grand wizardly gesture, spreading wide the cloak that wrapped him. He mantled like a hawk.

Something stirred against her foot. She jumped. "Stop that!" hissed Kerrec.

He looked as unconscious as ever, but he was right next to her; he had been halfway across the circle. Without magic she could not know what he meant to do.

"You have magic," he whispered, just loud enough for her to hear. "He tricked you, or you tricked yourself. Look."

Look inside, he meant. She wanted to say that she had looked, and there was nothing. Instead of looking she groped as if with hands, and found something. It was small and shivering and cold, but it was undoubtedly her magic.

Not that it could do much of anything inside the circle. Anything it tried would only rebound upon it, or go to feed the demon under the cloak.

"Take the Talisman," breathed Kerrec.

Rowan kicked him, surreptitiously she hoped, under her skirt. Was he serving the sorcerer after all?

"Take it," Kerrec whispered again. "I'm not the Byzantine's slave, damn it. I know what I'm doing. I'd do it myself if I could."

The sorcerer was screaming at her to take the thing. That was what she had been willing herself not to hear.

"Pretend," whispered Kerrec. "Let him think you obey him."

"No," she said, loud and clear. "I won't. I can't."

"Take it," they said together, one in a yowl, one in a hiss.

She would not.

Kerrec's hand darted out, plucked the cloak off the Talisman. Rowan leaped to stop him, but too late. She tripped over him and fell onto the hideous thing.

It beat under her like a heart. Her hand, which had been outstretched to break her fall, was caught under her, next to the burning metal. She scrambled to get up, to get away from it, but Kerrec's weight held her down.

He had her in a wrestler's hold, rather too much like some of the postures Rowan had seen Hrotrud in with certain of the young men of the palace. His breath was warm against her neck. His voice spoke in her ear. "Wrap your magic around it. Make a cloak or a veil, or anything that will wrap it and shield it."

The circle, she noticed distantly, was getting in Michael Phokias' way. He could not break it to get at them, not either easily or quickly. And if he did break it, he would set his demon free.

She could not think of anything better to do than what Kerrec said. A veil was easier to conceive of than a cloak. Silk, she thought, maybe grey, maybe green, maybe something of both. It billowed as she stretched it out with the hands of her magic, but then wound itself obediently about the demon-Talisman.

The demon tried to catch fire, but the veil prevented it, though some of the threads were scorched. Rowan wondered how long the silk could hold before the demon burned its way through.

"Now," said Kerrec, "I'm going to lift you up. Don't try to help me, and don't try to fight me. Just keep the demon from escaping."

His weight left her. He drew her up almost gently and set her on her feet, still with her back to him, and folded his arms about her middle. She was leaning lightly against him. They must have looked like a pair of lovers in a tryst.

"Hold up the Talisman," he said in the most unloverlike voice imaginable. It was shaking, for one thing. For another, it sounded furious.

That was only terror, and profound concentration. She felt it in him with what little of her magic she had to spare from trapping the demon. As she raised the Talisman on its chain, one of Kerrec's arms kept hold of her, and the other rose under her hands, helping them to bear the sudden weight.

It dragged at her, heavier the higher it rose, as if it was bound to the earth. She could lift it no more than heart-high. Then, even with Kerrec to help, she ran out of strength. She could hold it, but she could raise it no higher.

While the two of them struggled against the Talisman, Michael Phokias struggled to hurl his sorcery through the circle's walls. Rowan saw it as flashes of sudden light, or little lightnings, crackling and sparking on the wards that he himself had raised. None of it yet had come through.

Michael Phokias lowered his arms at last, as if in defeat. But Rowan knew better than to think he would give up so soon. His head bowed for a moment, then lifted. He spoke.

He put no music in the words, and no discord. He simply said them. They were not in any language Rowan knew or could guess at. They might have been nursery nonsense.

The power in them made the earth quiver. The Talisman jerked in her hands.

"Now," said Kerrec clearly, and not to Rowan. *"Now."*

A cloud raced across the moon. Darkness fell, darker than it should ever be, darkness absolute. Out of it came darkness deeper yet, and silence that shattered in the blare of a trumpet.

The moon's light flowed back again. It was cleaner, somehow; brighter, if only because the darkness had been so black.

Abul Abbas had come at last. He stood among the apple trees, as tall as they and broader by far. In the moon's absence he had been darkness made flesh. In the moon's splendor he was white unmarred, and his tusks were blades of light. High above his head in the snake's coil of his trunk struggled a small and gibbering thing that, with numbed slowness, Rowan recognized as Michael Phokias.

His gibbering had power in it, but it fell unheeded on the Elephant's head, dripped and ran and transmuted from blood-dark to glistening bright.

"Thank every god there is," Kerrec said. He let Rowan go, stepping past her, striking the circle's wall with his fist. It shattered and fell in shards like glass.

Rowan cried out. "No! The demon—you've set it free!"

He had not. It was still in her hands, bound with its chain. She dared not leave the circle, broken or no. She dared not even move.

Michael Phokias twisted in the Elephant's grip. Something flashed: the blade of a knife. It stabbed the sensitive trunk. Abul Abbas squealed, piercingly high, and dashed him down.

In the same instant, the Talisman wrenched at Rowan's hands. She wrenched back. Inside her, something snapped. She swung the thing up—it was weightless suddenly, as light as air—and then down. Even as Michael Phokias fell, the Talisman struck the earth.

The ground heaved. Rowan fell to her knees and clung to the grass, as the world did its best to buck her from its back.

Abul Abbas stamped. The earth trembled one last time and went still. Very slowly, very unsteadily, Rowan wobbled to her feet.

Kerrec was stumbling up, too. Which one of them

moved first, she never did discover. It seemed perfectly sensible to stagger together and cling, and stare stupidly at something that gleamed in the grass.

Gold, white, red, green, and the glitter of crystal under the moon. The Talisman was itself again. The demon was gone.

The spell was broken. Rowan sensed no taint or stain of it, anywhere that her magic could reach.

Sixteen

VICTORY could have been more obvious.

Michael Phokias was not dead. He was stunned and his arm was broken, but he had not had the good grace to die when the Elephant flung him down. Rowan handed him over to her father's guards, tied up bodily with strips torn from her shift, and bound in mind and magic with a spell that Kerrec knew. Both would hold him, she hoped, until she—or better yet her father—could decide what to do with him. The guards' eyes were full of questions, but they did not ask any of them. They looked at Rowan's face and went white, and did as she commanded.

The sorcerer was taken, the Talisman returned to the light again, but nothing had changed in the palace. Neither Gisela nor the Emperor showed any immediate signs of waking. Rowan and Kerrec between them put Gisela back to bed, where they found Gisela's erstwhile guards sound asleep, with no memory when they woke of doing anything but keeping vigil through a quiet night. Rowan did not try to explain. She was desperate to find her father up and yelling for his breakfast.

But he was doing no such thing. He lay as he had lain for these long awful days, with lamps at head and foot as if for the dead, and a lone priest praying over him.

Rowan sat in the chair by the bed, too tired even to cry.

Kerrec touched her arm. "I should see to Abul Abbas," he said in a low voice. "The Greek cut him with that knife, not badly, but I should tend the wound."

Rowan shrugged. Let him go. What did he matter? Her father was going to die.

Kerrec hovered, shifting from foot to foot. "Sometimes these things take time. Maybe by morning—"

"Go away," said Rowan.

"I'll come back as soon as I can," Kerrec said. He sounded strange, as if he was refraining from snapping at her.

"Don't," she said. "Just go."

He wavered for a while longer, but then he went. Rowan stayed where she was. Her father's face was unchanged in the lamps' light. The priest stopped praying, eyed her curiously, crossed himself and mumbled something about the privy.

Bless his percipience. Rowan tucked up her feet and leaned her head against the chair's high back. Her eyelids sank under their own weight.

Rowan started out of a dream in which she rode a white elephant on the back of a white aurochs under a moon that was a demon's eye. Somebody was swearing in gutter Frankish, language that would have made a guardsman blush.

The Emperor's bed was surrounded by vultures, black-winged things that flapped and squawked. Rowan grabbed hold of the first thing that came to hand and waded in, beating off the carrion birds.

Consciousness came abruptly. She stood beside the great bed, with the flock of doctors flapping for safety, and her father bolt upright, damning them to every hell in the trooper's canon.

She stared at what she held. It was the Talisman on its chain. But she had given it to Kerrec, and he had tied it up in Gisela's cloak and hidden it in the Elephant's house.

Without even thinking, she climbed up on the bed and dropped the chain over her father's head. He was still consigning the whole race of doctors to perdition; he barely noticed what she did until she had done it. He blinked and came into focus.

"Theoderada?" he said.

She nodded. Her throat, for some reason, was tight.

He looked down at himself in his shirt like a grave-shroud, and round at the lamps and the room reeking of incense and medicines, and frowned. "I've been sick, I take it."

She nodded again.

"And you let the doctors at me?"

He was building up a fine fit of temper. She halted it with one of her own. "How could *I* stop them? I was asleep!"

"Shirker." But his eyes were glinting. "Very well, I forgive you." And, somewhat alarmed: "There, little bird. There now. There."

He never did know what to do with women who burst without warning into tears. Or maybe after all he did. Holding her and patting her and telling her "There now" was as much as anyone could do.

Dammed-up tears were the worst kind. They took forever to pour out, and they hurt. But it was a good hurt, and her father was there to make it better.

The explanations took even longer than the tears had. Rowan did not know if her father understood all of it, or believed it. He listened, at least, and did not interrupt her even when she ran out of breath and started hiccoughing, and needed a swallow of wine to get her going again.

When it was all told, Rowan sat in her father's lap like the child she no longer was, and waited for him to say something. Anything.

"That's the truth, you know," said Abbess Gisela.

She looked as fresh as the morning, which for a fact it was: Rowan stared numbly at the grey light creeping through the windows. She was not smiling, but there was a light of gladness in her that even her stern expression could not dim.

The Emperor regarded his sister with some bemusement and a great deal of respect. "So, then. You share these moonlight fancies?"

"Moonlight's in them, certainly," the abbess said, "but they happened if she says they did. She's Fastrada's child, Carl. Are you going to tell yourself that doesn't mean what you know it means?"

Rowan eased herself out of her father's lap and stood

up stiffly. If she was to be named a witch, she wanted to be on her feet for it.

He seemed not to be aware of her, or of anything but his sister. His hand rose seemingly of its own accord and touched the Talisman, which was still hanging on his breast. It looked garish against the plainness of his shirt, its gold and jewels too bright, its crystal too large for symmetry.

Rowan's breath caught. There was nothing there but gold and jewels and a splinter of relic. No magic at all. "We broke it," she said, almost ready to cry again. "We took the demon out of it, but we didn't know to put the magic back."

"It's still a relic," Abbess Gisela said, "and valuable. Do you think he'll need it again as it was?"

"The sorcerer's still alive," Rowan said. She turned toward the door, ready to run and make sure that he had not suborned his guards or wrought a spell and escaped.

"He's alive, is he?" said the Emperor. "I'll see him, then. And then we'll see."

"But," Rowan said. "You've been ill—you can't—"

He most certainly could. A man who had been ill for days should have been weak and helpless, but Carl had fallen victim to sorcery. Magic had brought him back, and magic made him strong. He had his breakfast as he liked to have it, to his servants' astonishment and deep delight, good plain food and plenty of it, and then he swam in his baths, to be clean. And when he was entirely restored to himself, he dressed as he liked to dress, in the good plain clothes of a Frankish nobleman, and put

177

the Talisman back on again. He did not care that it had lost its magic. It was holy enough by itself, and would protect him. Rowan wished he had been that sensible when it was first given to him.

So cleaned and clothed and protected, he had the sorcerer brought to him.

The Emperor had taken it into his head to address the malefactor in the place where he had worked his sorceries. The grass of the orchard was still stained and trampled with the marks of the night's struggle. While he waited for the prisoner to be brought out, he paced, taking note of the charred and broken circle, the impress of bodies in it, the deep marks of the Elephant's feet.

Away under the trees he stooped and lifted a knife with a blade like black glass, a wicked-looking thing even in the sunlight. Rowan cried out to see it in his hand.

Even as he brought the knife back to the circle, the Talisman seemed to drink the sun, casting sparks of gold and red and blue and green. No magic left, no, but power enough of its own kind. Rowan was slightly comforted; and more so when her father handed the black knife to one of his guards. The man took it gingerly and held it for a while, until he got over his fear of what it was and thrust it into his belt.

Through all of this, there were other people there, as always where the Emperor was: his guards, a clerk or two, the priest who had kept vigil in the night. They were all as close to singing as they dared come, Rowan suspected; the younger or brasher ones kept breaking out in grins. Only Abbess Gisela seemed perfectly in control of her face, sitting serenely under a tree, greeting with lifted brow the arrival of two newcomers.

They were impossible to miss. The Elephant paced among the trees, with Kerrec riding on his neck. Abul Abbas was wearing his golden harness in the Emperor's honor, and the golden knobs on the tips of his tusks, but not the house that lordlings liked to ride in. He looked impossibly splendid.

He was also still more white than grey. His hide was silvery rather than ashen pale, with a sheen that maybe only Rowan—and Kerrec—could see. Wonder unfolded in her. Here, she knew all at once, was where the magic had gone. She liked it much better embodied in Abul Abbas than in the cold metal of the Talisman.

The Emperor paused on the charred edge of the circle. He was always delighted to see the Elephant, a delight like a child's. When Abul Abbas offered the tip of his trunk, Carl took it and bowed. "My Lord Elephant," he said. The Elephant dipped his great jeweled head. Everyone stared, except Kerrec, who was looking smug.

Rowan wanted to drag him off the Elephant's neck and demand to know what he thought he was doing. Since she could not reach that high, she settled for a smoldering stare. Kerrec was up to something. It had to do with the Emperor, and with the sorcerer, and it was probably reprehensible.

She was thoroughly startled when, having paid his respects to the Emperor, Abul Abbas turned toward her. His trunk was round her waist before she knew what he had done, lifting her in a giddy arc and depositing her, breathless and just beginning to shake, on his neck in front of Kerrec.

There was just room enough for both of them. It was not dignified at all. And it was a long, long way to the ground.

Now everyone was staring at her. Her cheeks were burning hot. She did not know what expression Kerrec wore, but she could feel him behind her, as stiff as she, and quite as nonplussed.

Fortunately the guards came before anyone could say anything, bringing a draggled figure wrapped in chains. Michael Phokias by daylight was not imposing to look at, with his clothes torn and stained and his arm bound up in a sling, his face bruised above the matted beard and his head bare of its perennial hat. He was bald on top. He seemed to be ashamed of that; he kept turning as if to hide it.

The Emperor sat on a stool that one of the guards had brought, throne enough for any battlefield. And so this was. The Emperor sat as victor, the sorcerer faced him as the vanquished, and whatever mercy there might be was for the Emperor to bestow.

The guards brought the prisoner to face the Emperor, and stood back in a circle. Rowan, high up on the Elephant's neck, saw easily over the heads of the tallest.

Carl began mildly, conversationally, without flourishes. "I hear alarming things of you, sir ambassador." He gestured round about. "Is this your work?"

Michael Phokias went down on his knees. If he had thought of groveling on his face as Byzantines did in front of their emperors, one of the guards prevented it, pulling his chain up short and holding him where he was. He sighed, shrugged, as if to say that it did not matter. "My Lord of the Franks, is there any defense that you will hear, or am I tried and sentenced in my absence?"

Rowan's fingers tightened on the stiff embroidery of the Elephant's harness. Before she could open her mouth to protest, her father said, "No, no Greekeries here, sir ambassador. We're Franks; we speak bluntly. Did you do this?"

"I did not," said the Byzantine, brazenly bold.

"Then," said Carl, "who did?"

Michael Phokias pointed with his chin, since his hands were bound. "Those, my lord of the Franks. The elephant and its keepers."

Rowan was mute with fury. Kerrec, perhaps unfortunately, was not. "Certainly we did the worst of it, sire," he said. "The circle, however, is his. Likewise the reason for the rest. He worked magics to destroy you and your daughters."

"You would know of magic, would you not, young warlock?" said Michael Phokias, all sweet poison.

"Oh, I am a Breton and a witch," Kerrec admitted freely, "but I never worked black magic in my life."

Rowan tried to kick him, but it was too awkward with him behind her. He went right on digging his own pit. "You won't talk your way out of this one. Your magic is gone; his majesty is immune to it in any case, and his patience has its limits."

"And who are you," the Byzantine inquired, "to speak for the royal will?"

"I could ask that myself," the Emperor said. His

mild voice was a relief after the other two, which had been clashing like blades. "I knew my elephant had a boy to tend him, but not that the boy was Breton. Who was letting me think that you were one of the Caliph's people?"

Of course Kerrec had to answer him directly. "Why, sire, I did, if you mean that I made no effort to enlighten you. I didn't see that it mattered. I'd be the Elephant's boy if I were Breton or Frank or Greek."

"Magic," somebody muttered.

"Why, yes," said Kerrec. "He's a very magical beast, is Abul Abbas. Elephants are. It's their nature."

Carl was intrigued, but his patience was not infinite. Just before Rowan expected him to erupt, Kerrec shut up. So, for a miracle, did the Byzantine. Carl working himself into a temper was a fearsome sight.

"I see," he said at length, his voice as soft as ever, but Rowan shivered. She prayed that Kerrec would stay quiet and let the Byzantine hang himself.

"I see," the Emperor said again, "that there is much that I've been omitting to observe. My fault, I'm sure. Is there a particular reason why an ambassador of the noble Empress Irene would be wishing to dispose of me by means as foul as they were unusual?"

"The Empress is dead," said Michael Phokias. "I serve the most sublime and noble Emperor Nikephoros, may he live ten thousand years."

"Ah," said Carl. There was a world of understanding in the word. "Poor Irene. Was it poison? Or a knife in her sleep? Or maybe a bit of magic?"

"That is not given me to know," Michael Phokias said stiffly. Rowan realized that he honestly did not know, and that he felt it as an insult.

"Ah well," the Emperor said, sighing. "Whatever the cause, she's dead, and your putative embassy is no longer possessed of its excuse. Is there any reason why I shouldn't have the lot of you whipped naked from my empire?"

"No," said Michael Phokias, still stiff. "Except perhaps that the others did not know what I knew. They approached you in good faith. I am the only one, as yet, who knowingly serves Nikephoros."

"And serving him, you tried to kill me. You'll die for that."

Carl said it calmly. Michael Phokias took it with almost equal calm. "Am I allowed to choose the manner of my death?"

"Not if you expect to trick your way out of it," said Carl.

Michael Phokias smiled thinly. Rowan had to admire him for his courage, even if he might still think he could escape. He was what her father would have called a worthy enemy.

He kept on smiling, and he said, "Very well, I am generous; I yield the choice to you. I only ask that it be quick."

The Emperor nodded. He rose; he plucked the sword from a guard's scabbard. Michael Phokias just had time to widen his eyes before the Emperor cut him down.

Seventeen

· · · · · · · · · · · · ·

T HERE WAS an enormous silence. They had all seen death before, as they had seen justice, and often together. But this was the justice of the battlefield, swift, sudden, and without appeal.

Rowan stared at her father. He had done this before. She had heard the stories; she had watched him slay the boar. But to see him kill a man . . . that was different.

He sank to one knee beside Michael Phokias. His face had its king-look, cold and still. He closed the staring eyes, paused with his hand on the man's forehead, and sighed. "God have mercy on us."

The priest echoed him. No one else did. The Emperor rose more stiffly than he had knelt, moving for a moment like an old man, until he remembered himself. The guard reclaimed his bloodied sword and began to wipe it on the grass. Others, moving with quiet efficiency, bore the body away out of sight if not, for a long while, out of mind.

There was blood on the Emperor's hand. Abbess Gisela wiped it off with her own veil, not saying anything; not shrinking, either.

"He doesn't feel anything," Rowan said to herself. "Not a thing."

"Yes, he does," said Kerrec at her back.

She could not safely round on him on that perch; she settled for a sharp word. "No."

"Theoderada," said Kerrec with all the weariness in the world, "won't you stop contradicting me at every hint of opportunity and *listen* for once? Of course he feels this man's death, as he feels every other death he's meted out since he became a man and a king. He can't stop deal,ing justice just because it hurts. That man earned hissentence. He got as easy a one as mortal sinner everhad."

"Too easy," said Rowan with sudden fierceness. "My father shouldn't have stained his hands."

"Oh, shouldn't he?"

She twisted her head to glare at him, but he was gone, sliding down the Elephant's side.

Cursing every trick of men and elephants, she slid as Kerrec had, but without the grace. The Elephant's trunk held her up as she started to fall; it lowered her carefully to the ground, face to face with Kerrec.

She turned her back on him. That turned her outward toward the rest of the world. Her aunt was standing just out of the Elephant's reach, looking more amused than not.

"Gisela's herself again," the abbess said, as if that was all she had come to say. "She woke up this morning, somewhat before your father did, with no memory of anything that happened after sunset yesterday."

"That's a mercy," said Kerrec. "And before sunset? Does she remember her bewitchment?"

"I think not," the abbess said. "She's a little indisposed this morning, but then she often is. She'll have to learn to dispense with that if she expects to survive the discipline of a convent."

"I don't think she ever will," Rowan said. Her temper was cooling, whether it wished to or no. It often did in front of the abbess. "She has dreams. All the Emperor's daughters do. But we can't be anything but princesses."

"Even you?" Kerrec asked.

She spun. He was not visibly making fun of her. His eyes were wide and level and bright, but not with mockery.

She answered him straight, and let her temper find its own way out. "I as much as any. Isn't that what you were trying to teach me?"

"I was trying to teach you to be Theoderada. Who is Rowan. Who is anyone she wants to be."

"Except a plain man's wife, with no magic in her."

"Oh, you could be that," said Kerrec. "You only have to want it badly enough."

Her heart thudded. She was aware of her aunt, listening but not speaking, and of the Elephant, standing like a wall behind them, and of the sun over them, growing warm as it rose toward noon.

And of her father. He had left the place of his justice and come round the wall that was the Elephant, and stood listening as the rest of them did.

Words died in her throat.

"Do you want that?" her father asked. "Do you really want that of all things in the world?"

Yes, Rowan tried to say. But her tongue was numb. She stared at the Talisman on his breast. There was another on hers, invisible but as heavy as the world, and its name was magic. She could use it one last time, to make her father give her what she wanted; then give it up, cast it away, be nothing more or less than Rowan.

"No," she said. "No, I don't want it, any more than Gisela really wants the convent. I'd be bored silly in a week."

"I don't suppose," her father said, "you want to be that man's wife."

She looked around in incomprehension. "What man?" Then she saw the flush on Kerrec's cheeks, and felt her own rising to match it.

He was the one, this time, who said, "No. You don't want me."

"And why not?" Rowan demanded, grandly contrary.

"I'm only the Elephant's boy. I have no lands, no honor—"

"Nonsense!" Rowan snapped. "Father, do you know who he is?"

"Am I supposed to guess?" the Emperor inquired. "What is he, one of Roland's kin?"

"Yes," said Rowan.

Carl's face lit with pleasure. "Why, boy, why didn't you say so? What were you trying to do, play some outland game of proving yourself worthy in spite of your family? Roland tried that on me once, he and Oliver. Took me the damnedest time to see through it."

Kerrec had gone an interesting shade of crimson. Finally the Emperor paused for breath, and Kerrec could get a word in edgewise. "No! Did you hear me, sire? I have no honor."

"But how can a kinsman of Roland's be without honor?" Then Carl's brow furrowed. Rowan watched him remember. "No. No, I never believed it, in spite of what everyone said. So you're Count Everard's boy, are you? I'd heard he had a son, but they said you were dead. Else I'd have sought you out."

"And when would you have done that, my lord Emperor?" asked Kerrec. "You have a whole empire to think of. Brittany is the merest appendage, its people more rebellious than complaisant."

"So you thought you'd try me from behind, did you, then?"

Kerrec kept his head up, which was more than Rowan could have managed. "I thought I'd earn my way as I could, and if you honored me, then I would return that honor to my father."

"You should have come straight to me," the Emperor said.

"I thought of it," said Kerrec. "But what if you believed our enemy? Everyone else did. Then what would I have? This way I had the Elephant, and respect enough to go on with."

"And my daughter?"

Black eyes met blue ones. "I doubt that your daughter has ever uttered a civil word to me. Are the stories false, after all, that you don't allow them husbands? Are you trying to marry her off?"

Carl's mustache bristled. His eyes blazed. Suddenly,

with no warning at all, he laughed. He laughed loud and he laughed long, and he did not care in the least that no one else laughed with him.

When he could talk again, he had to do it in bursts, through new gusts of mirth. "I see," he said, "that you know my Rowan. Prickly, isn't she? We should have named her Thornbush. And do you like her, then?"

"Do I dare?"

Carl grinned like a wolf, a grin that matched Kerrec's. It was quite beyond bearing.

Rowan thrust herself between them. "Stop that, you two! I'm not a mare you're chaffering over."

Their grins did not even waver. She glared at them both. "Well, Father? Are you going to give him his honor back, and give us all some peace?"

"Honor," said the Emperor, "and lands, and all else that he has lost."

Kerrec looked faintly winded by his good fortune, but he would never give up his grin for that.

"And you," Rowan said to him. "Why in the world would I want you for anything but a friend?"

That wiped the grin off his face.

"Friends can be lovers," Abbess Gisela observed. "Eventually. When they outgrow their very natural urge to kick and squeal at one another."

Rowan was blushing again. So was Kerrec. And her father was going to collapse if he laughed much harder.

She had enough wits left to make sure of one thing at least. "Kerrec has his honor back? Your word on it, Father?"

"My word and my bond," he said. "Everything that was taken from him, he shall have again."

"But," said Kerrec, "what if I don't want it?"

"Of course you want it," said Rowan. "You've spent your whole life trying to get it."

"No," said Kerrec. "I've spent my life trying to get my honor back. If I have that, I don't care what else I have. I'd rather stay here and serve the Elephant and be simply Kerrec, than be a lord in Brittany."

"You children are two of a kind," Abbess Gisela observed.

"And why," demanded Rowan, ignoring her, "can't you have both? You can be a lord and look after Abul Abbas. I don't see why you have to be so difficult about it."

He was going to be even more difficult, she could see. But her father headed him off. "Why, young lord, if it pleases your fancy to be the Elephant's boy, then so you shall be. He likes you, even I can see that. But you won't escape the rest of it. Honor costs, sir. It never comes free."

Even Kerrec could see the truth of that. Maybe Abul Abbas helped him: the Elephant's trunk slithered over his shoulder and curled around his body, as if to keep him from escaping.

He managed not to look too terribly trapped. After all, the Elephant was what he wanted. He could evade the rest of it without excessive trouble, as long as he had Abul Abbas to hide behind.

"It won't be so bad," the Emperor said, "to have a

name and possessions and a place in the world apart from my lord Elephant. If nothing else, you'll be able to afford a new coat."

Kerrec shrugged in his old and ragged one. He was trying to be nonchalant, but Rowan could see the joy bubbling up in him as the truth of it finally struck him.

It had taken long enough. She met the Elephant's eye. He was laughing at them all.

And no wonder. They had yattered so much, only to end up back where they started. The Emperor was as hearty as ever, Gisela her mooncalf self, Kerrec restored to his name and his honor.

As for Rowan, she had magic, singing in her, and a friend who was an elephant, and—yes—one who was a Breton witch. He would look well in scarlet silk. She knew just the bolt she would cut it from. And if he objected, why then, she would remind him that he was a lord again at last, but she was a princess, and he must do as she commanded. That would put him in a right temper.

Somewhere in the air, she felt her mother's presence. It was a little warmer than the sun, and it glimmered among the apple boughs. It did not linger long. Just long enough for her to know that it was there; to touch the Emperor with a whisper of breeze, ruffling his hair; and to pause before the Elephant, bowing to his great magic and wisdom. Then, like a breeze, it was gone.

The Elephant raised his trunk as if in farewell, then lowered it gently to rest on Rowan's shoulder. She glanced at Kerrec, who stood on her other side. He laid a hand on the Elephant's trunk, as if to close their circle.

Rowan knew a moment's urge to fling herself away from them both. But she stayed where she was. It was, not comfortable, no, but somehow *right*.

The Elephant's eye caught hers. As clearly as she had ever heard her mother's voice, she knew what he was telling her. *Is it better, then, than being simply Rowan?*

"No," said Rowan, too quickly. But then her tongue caught up with the rest of her. "Yes," she said in wonder. "Yes, it is. Who'd ever have thought it?"

Who indeed? said the Elephant.

She could not tell if he was laughing. After a moment she decided that it did not matter. A moment more, and she was laughing, too, laughter that let the sunlight in and drove all the dark away.

"For a while," said Kerrec, reading her as easily as letters on a parchment.

A while is long enough, said the Elephant.

Postlude

*I*N THE WORLD we know, Abul Abbas did not live three hundred years as people had been expecting that he would, or even the fifty that would be usual for an elephant. He died in the year 810, eight years after he was brought to Aachen. Germany was too cold and wet for him, and he never quite recovered from the rigors of his journey from the east. His death was much mourned. He had been one of the great wonders of Charlemagne's realm, the only elephant in the west of the world.